Alibis & Alchemy

Potion Shop Intern

Book 1

LUCINDA HARRISON

Alibis & Alchemy

Copyright © 2025 by Lucinda Harrison

ISBN: 978-1-7367596-6-0

*To my writing community, who supported
me from beginning to the very end.*

One

I STOOD BEFORE the wooden door to the corner shop and tightened the buckle on my cinched belt with my free hand. A worn carpetbag was clutched in the other, threadbare and dusty, filled with my worldly possessions, which were few: two spare socks—mismatched of course—an old plastic comb missing three teeth, a ragged book of short stories that I'd read through a thousand times, along with a few scraps of clothing I'd collected over the years.

In totality, I was not much to consider—average height with shoulder-length brown hair, rough-cut and held back in a low, stumpy ponytail. Ms. Ruthie, headmistress at the orphanage, had told me I blended into the background of any room, even if I was standing square in the middle. I didn't think it was meant as a compliment.

But despite my oversized and mismatched clothes, bland appearance, and minimal possessions, there I stood, ready to take on a new adventure. I could hardly believe my luck when Ms. Ruthie had handed me a letter and told me the American Association of Potion Masters had selected me for an internship.

"It's *dumb* luck," Ms. Ruthie had said to me. "Pure dumb luck."

My fingers had trembled, and I read the letter three times through before I understood what it meant. In a month's time, I'd be a bona fide potion-making intern, mixing magical concoctions and learning the ins and outs of a real profession.

Seventeen long years at the local orphanage could make one think there was little to look forward to in life. I had only one short year until the clock ran out on finding a family and living off the purse of social services. The gaping chasm of the unknown loomed on my horizon, and I'd likely be shunted into a role as caretaker at the orphanage, working for Ms. Ruthie. Forever. My stomach roiled at the thought.

Shaking it off, I pulled the Association's letter from my pocket and unfolded it with delicate fingers. I scanned the words once more, just to be sure it hadn't been a dream or a prank or a misunderstanding, and actually, Carmody Greene, you'll be joining the other washed-up orphans at the factory for Crazy Barry's Bargain Basement Brooms.

With a relieved sigh, I refolded the letter along the fraying seams and returned it to my pocket. This internship could be the opportunity I needed to break from an inevitable life of dullness and drudgery. The only thing standing between me and a magical new existence was a worn, yet sturdy wooden door attached to a corner building held together by old bricks and swaths of thick moss.

Above the street corner a few yards away, a round turret jutted from the building's upper floors and loomed over the sidewalk, threatening to collapse at any moment.

Carefully, timidly, I reached for the door handle. The gentle tinkle of the door chime sounded as I took my first step inside the potion shop.

My head spun at the array of jars and jugs, phials and flasks, and walls lined with a rainbow of tonics and tinctures. The early morning light glinted off the colorful bottles, casting a prism onto the otherwise plain walls of the shop. A mix of scents wafted through the air—sage and sulfur and cinnamon and many more I couldn't quite place. It was like a dream. A magical, whimsical dream.

Two gray-haired heads popped up from behind a display case. I blinked. Were they twins? Other than their identical faces, their appearances couldn't have been further from one another. While one had a long, delicate braid that cascaded over one shoulder and kind, smiling eyes, the other let her frizzy hair flow wild, and one brown eye twitched as she gave me a stern once-over.

"H-hello," I said. "I'm Carmody Greene, your new intern. I hope I'm not too early."

The stink-eyed twin flinched. "Our what?"

"Intern?" the kind-looking one repeated. Bewilderment blinked back at me. "Whatever do you mean, my dear?"

My stomach sank. *Am I in the wrong place?* My eyes flicked to the sign in the window, and I read it under my breath. "Meriweather Potions, Tingle Level Ten Potion Masters, A.A.P.M., S.I.P.P." There was no mistaking that this was the right shop, corner of Main Street and Cobblestone Way.

I fumbled for the letter, less gently this time in my haste, and passed it to the braided woman with a trembling hand. "I'm supposed to start today. Aren't you expecting me?"

The one with unkempt hair peered over the other's shoulder. "What's it say, Esme?"

Esme let out a small gasp. "It's from the Association. I can't believe they didn't warn us." She spared me a glance and a weak smile. "Nothing on you, dear, but this is rather unexpected."

The other woman frowned and squinted as if trying to recall a memory.

"What is it?" Esme asked her. When her twin didn't respond, she repeated more firmly, "Henny, what is it?"

Henny's eyes dipped low. "There may have been a letter."

Esme's mouth dropped open. "What do you mean 'There may have been a letter'?"

Henny waved a hand toward a counter against the far wall, where a stack of papers lay haphazard and forgotten. "About a month ago. I never opened it. Assumed it was one of those annoying donation requests they're always sending."

Esme rushed to the counter and flipped through the papers, tossing aside HVAC mailers and political flyers, then held up an unopened envelope with the Association's bold logo emblazoned on the front. With worry on her face, she ripped it open, leaving a ragged tear, and pulled out a single sheet of crisp white paper. She cleared her throat.

"The American Association of Potion Makers wishes to congratulate Esmeralda and Henrietta Meriweather on your recent achievement of Tingle Level Ten Potion Masters. As newly appointed potion masters, it is your obligation not only to provide potions of the highest

potency, quality, and caliber, but also to serve as ambassadors and mentors for the Association's next generation of potion masters."

Henny eyed me again. "I don't much like obligations."

I swallowed down the lump that rose in my throat and pictured returning to the orphanage, the smug look on Ms. Ruthie's face as I slunk inside, tail between my legs, thoroughly humiliated. Who was I to think I could have something wonderful?

"There's more," Esme said, then continued reading aloud.

"The Association strives to ensure our most disadvantaged youth have opportunities to thrive and acquire valuable skills in the most in-demand trades in hopes that, upon maturity, they may transition into successful members of society. As such, you will be required to take under your tutelage an intern from the nearest public orphanage."

Henny grumbled. "I take it you're our orphan."

My excitement at this point had completely deflated, like a balloon left to sputter all its air and then sink to the ground, totally flattened. They weren't expecting me. They weren't prepared for me. And the squirrelly-eyed one definitely didn't want me.

Esme looked up from the letter and then at me. "It's all right, dear. We're taken a bit by surprise, that's all. The letter goes on.

"Continued membership in the Association is contingent upon completion of the six-month internship. During this time, you will house, feed, and instruct said intern in the basics of the potion-making craft and business. A

complete curriculum may be accessed on the Association's website. Each month, an Association compliance officer will visit to ensure the collaboration continues to be a positive and effective experience for all parties. Should you have any questions, you may reach out to our Youth Internship Program between the business hours of nine a.m. and five p.m., Monday through Friday. Please make all necessary preparations as your intern will arrive on the first day of May."

Henny grimaced as Esme finished reading, the wrinkles around her mouth deepening.

Esme shook the page at Henny. "We should have opened this weeks ago." She lowered her voice to a whisper. "We have to house her, feed her. The entire upstairs is in shambles, and she's going to live here. With *us*."

"We can send her back," Henny said, not trying to keep her voice low.

I clutched my carpetbag tighter. *Not back. Please not back.*

"Good heavens, don't be ridiculous," Esme said, sparing me a look. "Besides, our membership requires it. Perhaps we should make the best of it."

Henny waved a hand at the letter. "Then I'll call this Youth Internship Program. Clear it all up. Get an extension." Her eyes lit up. "Better yet, an *exemption*."

I cried out inside. *Please, no.*

Esme bobbed her head my way. "It's the first of May. She's already here."

Henny grunted, ruminated, then let out a heaving sigh, which I sincerely hoped meant she had conceded to the arrangement. "All right, then," she said, "let's take a look at you." She crossed her arms and gave me an appraising once-over, frowning at my oversized pants cinched tightly at the waist. "What was your name again?"

"Carmody Greene."

"And how old are you?"

"Seventeen, ma'am."

"None of that ma'am business. I'm Henny. This is Esme, my twin sister, as you've probably gathered."

Esme's face beamed with a warm, grandmotherly smile. "We're so pleased to have you."

"There will be rules in this household," Henny said. "Strict rules. We run a tight ship. You don't get to be Tingle Level Ten Potion Masters by flouncing around with your head in the clouds."

I nodded, thanking my stars they'd abandoned the idea of sending me back to Ms. Ruthie. "I understand. And thank you for accepting me into your home. I hope to make you proud and one day join the Association to be a Potion Master like both of you."

Henny jutted out her chin and gave one curt nod. "Too right."

Esme approached and wrapped an arm around my shoulder. "Why don't you set down your bag and we'll give you a little tour? You'll have to excuse the mess. We weren't expecting—"

Henny sputtered a conspicuous cough. "Aren't you forgetting something, Esme?"

Esme appeared confused, then shook her head. "Of course. Chief Rat."

"Chief Rat." Henny repeated the words with contempt. "If my suspicions are correct, he's due for one of his *surprise* inspections today. He can bring his worst, but

I'm ready. I won't be some floppity pushover this time."

Esme sighed. "Since when have you ever been a floppity pushover?"

"Who is Chief Rat?" I asked.

Esme patted me on the arm. "Don't you worry about that, dear."

Henny rounded on me. The eye twitch had returned. "Chief Rat is the most despicable, diabolical, unscrupulous code inspector to stalk the streets of Chester Hollow."

"Code inspector?"

"Regulations and Town Standards," Esme said. "He's the chief inspector."

"R.A.T.S.," Henny said with a snarl. "Chief Rat is always sniffing around, always finding a way to burrow into your last nerve. Last time, he turned up during my morning constitutional. Well, I won't be caught with my pants down today." She let out a satisfied grunt.

"Perhaps we should get Carmody settled in and then we can—"

The door swung open, and the bells clanged sharply from the force.

"Meriweather Potions," a slithery voice said, "prepare for your spot inspection."

* * *

If rats walked among us, this man personified one of those furry vermin. Squinty eyes and an elongated snout of a nose, he bobbed his head as though sniffing the air. *Wait, was he sniffing the air?*

"Smells like sulfur, ladies," he said. "And that smells

like a violation to me." He pulled a notebook from the pocket of his vest—a striking, leather-bound pad in a lustrous marbled pattern—and scribbled a notation. "That's a repeat offense."

Henny puffed out her chest and stomped up to the man. "Give it a rest, Oliver. As I explained last time, that smell is from our line of boutique bathroom potions."

"Our Powder Room Potations collection," Esme interjected.

Henny wagged a finger toward Oliver. "And you know very well this property is coded for commercial potion-making."

He looked down his nose at the wild-haired woman. "That may be so, but *this* is certainly not up to code." Bending down, he plucked a vial of viscous green goo off the floor.

Esme scurried forward. "But we were just moving that from one case to the other when—" She paused and glanced at me. "When our new intern arrived."

His rat nose turned my way. I gulped back a lump of fear.

Henny snatched the vial from Oliver's hands and shoved it into a display case, then slid the glass door closed with a grunt. "Try again, *Mr. Oliphant.*"

I couldn't believe his eyes could narrow more than their previous squint, but they bored into Henny. "That's *Chief Inspector* to you."

She stood her ground, staring up at the much taller man, hands on her hips, defiant.

Suddenly, he spun. "Perhaps you haven't been so fastidious with your workroom."

He sauntered toward a doorway at the back of the

shop that was closed off with a flimsy fabric curtain. Brushing it aside, he stepped through, and the three of us followed, Henny stomping, Esme scurrying, and me bringing up the rear like a meek little mouse.

As I passed through the curtain, my mouth fell open at the sight. Bottles and jars and crumpled packets of who-knew-what lined the walls on floor-to-ceiling wooden shelves. I ran a hand along the nearest shelf and felt its time-worn smoothness and stared in wonder at the darkened patina of innumerable years of wear. Reaching out, I turned the closest bottle to read the label: Pickled Bunions. A gurgle escaped my lips as I jerked my hand away. The others showed no reaction. I supposed this was simply a supply room for them, an ordinary space for a potion-maker, creepy ingredients and all.

Other than the shelves, two sturdy work tables with accompanying stools sat on either side of the room, and in the center was an enormous fire pit, cold and unlit, but still impressive in its size. An exhaust pipe fitted ten feet over the pit led upward, through the ceiling and out of sight.

Oliver glanced around the room, rat nose still high in the air. "Those cauldrons there." He pointed to a shadowy corner where a tower of round metal pots was piled one atop the other. "That stack is a hazard." He jotted a few words in his notebook.

Henny waved a hand toward the pots. "Those are perfectly stacked stainless-steel cauldrons. You can't possibly think that's a problem. Look." She walked over and gave the pile a shove. They didn't budge.

Oliver pulled out a worn book from the same vest pocket, no bigger than the palm of his hand, and flipped through the thin pages before stopping midway. "Section fifty-two, paragraph seven of the *Regulations and Town Standards* states that unsecured cauldrons over twelve inches in diameter shall be stored in stacks of no more than…" He checked the verbiage again, eyes following down his nose at the text on the page. "Three."

"Oh dear," Esme whispered.

Henny shot her a scathing look. "Fine. I can fix that." She heaved all but three of the cauldrons off the stack and placed them in an open space on the floor nearby, then divided the stack again until there were no more than three to a pile.

Oliver tsked. "It appears there is now a violation of the accessibility and safety standards. Those cauldrons create a tripping hazard and block the avenues of egress."

Henny gritted her teeth. "Just go around you greasy—"

"Henny," Esme interjected in her sweet voice, "perhaps we can place the cauldrons in the storage closet under the stairs, out of everyone's way." She gave Oliver an acquiescing smile.

He sighed and made another notation. "I'll still have to cite it. I can't just pretend these violations didn't happen. It's my job, after all."

Esme leaned in and whispered to me, "If that's all he finds, we'll be getting off easy."

"Unfortunately," Oliver said, "there are a few more issues." He tapped his notebook with the pen, then shoved a hand into his pants pocket and pulled out a measuring tape. Crouching by the fire pit, he unfurled the measuring tape and squinted his beady eyes at the reading. One deep sigh and a scribble in his notepad later, he stood up to full height. "I'm afraid your ash pile is approximately two inches too high." He tsked again and shook his head. "When was the last time this was cleaned?"

"Yesterday," Henny blurted out, red-faced. "It was cleaned *yesterday*. What ridiculous, nonsensical, crack-brained violation is that?"

Oliver inclined his head ever so slightly, then glanced down at the palm-sized *Regulations and Town Standards* once again. The pages fluttered and then stopped. "Section fifty-six, paragraph nine. Honestly, ladies, a few more violations and you may need to close shop until you can get your business in order."

My eyes went wide. If the potion shop closed, what would that mean for my internship? I couldn't go back to the orphanage so soon. Ms. Ruthie would never let me live it down. "Sir," I sputtered. "I believe the Meriweathers were leaving the ash for me to clean up."

Henny and Esme exchanged surprised looks, and Oliver turned his rat-stare my way. I quickly dropped my eyes to look at the floor. Something told me this was a man who appreciated a heaping dose of docility.

I continued, "Safety is so important to both of them that it was going to be my first lesson."

He pursed his lips, clearly mulling this over.

Henny stepped to my side and placed an arm around my shoulder, giving me an exuberant squeeze. "Yes, yes. It's vital that young Carmody get a hands-on experience. As Potion Masters, it is our *obligation* to prepare this disadvantaged youth to become a successful member of society. We could yammer all day about mixing this and cleaning that, but getting your hands dirty? Pah, there's no better way to learn and grow."

Esme eased in and put her arm around my other shoulder. "Safety first, potions later."

Oliver eyed them suspiciously down his long nose. "I believe I've seen enough."

From the front room came the jingle of the door chime and a frilly, high-pitched, "Hello, anybody home?"

Henny gurgled under her breath.

"What's she doing here?" Esme scurried through the curtain, and we all followed suit.

A chipper woman, short and stout like a proud little bird, perched herself, arms crossed, against the front display case. "There you are," she said at the sight of us emerging from the back. "I was starting to think you'd gone out of business." Her expression widened at the sight of Oliver bringing up the rear. "Oh dear. Perhaps you have?" A faint upturn at the corner of her mouth belied her concern.

"Don't get so excited, Maude." Henny rolled the name from her mouth like a bit of rotten food. "He was just leaving, weren't you, Oliphant?"

Oliver raised one steely eyebrow, then tore a page from his notebook. "Continuous violations, ladies." He handed it to Esme, who took it from him with wilted acceptance. "Next time I won't be so understanding." He glanced my way, and his mouth twitched from side to side. "With a new intern present, I expect this establishment to adhere to all regulations and town standards. Failure will leave me with no option but to shut you down for good." In three broad strides he reached the door and exited the shop, leaving his last threat lingering in the air like moldy cheese.

"My, my," said Maude. "Sounds like that went

badly."

"Mind your own business," Henny snapped.

"Is there something we can help you with?" Esme asked. "Otherwise, we're quite busy and don't have time to chat."

Maude stretched her neck to see over the display case. "Did Mr. Oliphant say you had a new intern?"

I waved. "Hello. Nice to meet you. I'm—"

Henny shushed me with one wave of her hand. "What do you want, Maude? Isn't there some rock you need to slither under?"

Maude let out a chuckle. "You're always so funny. I'm here to ask if you'll be attending the mayor's big shindig tomorrow night. I hear it's always a blowout."

"If by blowout you mean obligatory attendance or face the wrath of R.A.T.S., then yes, a spectacular blowout."

"We're awfully busy," Esme said. "The mayor's gala may not be in the cards for us."

"And what about this new intern of yours? What was your name again?"

Caught off guard, I choked out a cough. "Carmody, ma'am."

"Carmody." Maude gave me an appraising look. "You must want to attend the biggest party of the year?"

I turned to Esme, uncertain of how to answer. Parties weren't a common occurrence at the orphanage. Non-existent, in fact. And I'd certainly never attended a gala.

"We'll see," Esme said.

Henny hiked up her pants. "As Tingle Level Ten Potion Masters, we've been granted the privilege of training the next generation of experts in the profession. There's quite a curriculum to get through. Not much time for galivanting and galas and all that."

Maude did not seem impressed. "I've got two staff of my own, you know."

"Pah! Your pimple-brained potion makers couldn't tingle their way out of a wide-mouthed cauldron."

At this, Maude bristled, showing a few cracks in her cheerful persona. "Elix Mix is a certified potion-making franchise. All employees are properly trained and—"

"Yes, yes," Henny interrupted. "Properly trained in the basics, I'm sure. The Meriweathers, however, we're in the business of expertise. And Carmody here will tingle circles around your *properly trained* staff."

"Oh, really?" Maude turned steely eyes to me. "Carmody, at what stage should essence of fleabane be added to a vial of freckle tonic?"

I froze. Fleabane? Freckle tonic? "Um, I'm not sure."

Henny rolled her eyes. "Don't be ridiculous, Maude. She started an hour ago."

Maude sauntered to the door, clearly pleased with herself. "Well, I hope she catches on fast. Oliver didn't seem too pleased, so you may not have much time left."

Red-faced, Henny yelled at the door as Maude slipped out, "Chief Rat can drop dead."

Two

AFTER THE MORNING'S excitement, Esme thought it a good idea to get me settled. She and Henny led me up a back stairwell, separate from the rest of the potion shop. Like the shelves, the stair treads and handrail glowed with the warm patina of time and repeated use.

"This building has been in the family for three generations. We've lived here our whole lives." Esme pointed to a picture hanging on the wall halfway up the stairs. Two cherub babes and a mischievous-looking toddler sat in a patch of grass surrounding an old woman perched on a simple stool. "That's our grandmother. She was a Potion Master, too."

I pointed to the fat babies. "Is that you and Henny?"

"What?" Henny scoffed in mock outrage. "Can't you tell by how adorable we are?"

"Yes," Esme replied. "That's us."

"Who's the other little girl?"

"That's our sister," Esme said. "We don't talk about her, though."

Curiosity let Esme's words fly right over my head.

"Why not?"

Henny scowled back at me on the lower step. "Didn't you hear what she just said? We don't talk about her."

I grimaced. "Sorry." I hadn't even made it up the stairs yet, so best not to ruffle anyone's feathers. They could still tell me to skedaddle and off to Crazy Barry's broom factory I would go.

"This is it," Esme said, opening a door at the top of the landing. "You'll have to forgive the mess. We weren't expecting company."

I followed the twins through to their living quarters, which opened into a broad room, dark from the heavy curtains and low ceiling.

Even through the dimness, I could tell the place was a disaster. Boxes, books, bras, bags, everything lay willy-nilly on the sparse and dusty furniture. A quick glance toward the kitchen area proved it was no better. It reminded me of Henny's messy mail pile in the shop downstairs.

Esme scuttled around the living room, tidying up as best she could. "Like I said, we didn't have time to straighten up. You must be shocked. It's normally not like this, though."

The layer of dust on the nearest side table told me differently. "It's okay," I said. "I cleaned all the time at the orphanage. I can take care of this for you."

Henny rubbed her hands together. "Excellent."

"Absolutely not." Esme frowned at Henny. "Carmody is our intern, not our housekeeper. We should be keeping a cleaner house, after all."

"But she offered."

"It's no trouble," I said. "Ms. Ruthie always had me

do the cleaning and the cooking. I also looked after the littlest ones who couldn't look after themselves, cleaned them and taught them their ABCs and all that. I changed the bedclothes, did the laundry and dishes, stocked the pantry, swept and mopped the floors and baseboards, dusted the lights, washed the windows. Gosh, that's all I can remember right now, but I'm sure there's more."

Henny's excitement had faded. "She made you do all that, this Ms. Ruthie? What the heck did *she* do?"

I thought for a moment, then realized I wasn't quite sure what Ms. Ruthie did. "Well, I guess she ran the orphanage."

The twins exchanged frowns.

"Don't you worry about tidying up," Esme said. "We'll take care of that. Should have happened a long time ago. But first, I should show you to your room. I'm afraid we have only one spare bedroom. I hope it's sufficient."

My own room? My fingers twitched at the handle of my bag. I could hardly contain my excitement. "I'm sure it will be wonderful. I shared with five other girls at the orphanage."

"Don't get excited until you see it," Henny said. "It's the old tower room."

I nearly chirped with glee. The *tower room*. How romantic. There was a poem in my little book about a woman who spends her time daydreaming in her high castle tower with a dozen cats and dogs. In the fleeting moments I'd had to read, that was the poem I always went back to, rereading it over and over and imagining a life of such leisure and luxury.

Another stairwell, this time curving upward to the

right, led to the tower room. Esme eased open the door cautiously, as though expecting something to jump out. When nothing did, she smiled and entered with tentative steps then immediately began pulling off the dusty furniture covers from their slumber.

"We don't use this room much," she said. "It's a bit too drafty in the winter, and I don't like to be this high up."

But I'd barely heard her. Upon entry, I gazed in wonder at the peaked ceiling with its array of beams twelve feet above my head. I guessed the room was about twelve feet in diameter, with stone-cobbled walls and three huge windows revealing a panorama of treetops and sky. It quickly dawned on me that I was in the very turret I'd spotted from the street. Despite looking like a stiff breeze may bring the whole thing down, it felt surprisingly sturdy under my feet. "This is amazing."

Esme tugged the dust cover off an iron bed frame. The metal springs creaked and groaned with even that slight a movement. She let out a few weak coughs as she folded the dust cover into a neat square and tucked it under one arm. "I'm glad you like it, dear. I know it's not much. And we'll make sure you get everything you need—extra blankets, that sort of thing."

I turned one window's hand crank, and it opened with an ear-splitting squeal as though sealed shut for an eternity. I peered down to the street below at the corner of Cobblestone and Main. Just a short time ago, I was standing down there, looking up at this very tower. "You can see everything from up here. Hey! There's a big sparkling dome over there." I pointed farther down the street where the sun glinted off the rounded roof of a far-off building.

Esme backed away. "Eh, yes. I'm not much of a fan of heights. Second-floor living is dangerous enough for me."

I pulled myself from the view and set my bag on the bed. *Squeak.* My bed. I hopped onto the mattress. *Squeak. Squeak.* A smile spread over my face. "I think I'm going to like it here."

* * *

Later that afternoon, after a few technical difficulties, Esme and Henny finally figured out the internship website and confirmed we were on track to begin my studies. They bustled me from the upstairs quarters down to the workroom where I was once again awed by the array of ingredients and potion-brewing paraphernalia.

A small wooden box sat atop one of the two worktables that flanked the room. Esme handed it to her twin, who tucked it under one arm.

"Before we get started on any formal instruction," Henny said, "we need to make a delivery to Astrid Starcaller. Normally, we'd take the tuk-tuk for deliveries, but it's just down the street. We should all go together this first time, show you how it's done and all that."

I nodded at her words, taking it all in. "What's a tuk-tuk?"

"Ever seen a rickshaw?" Henny asked. "Small motorized vehicle. Perfect size for deliveries. We don't need anything fancy like Elix Mix's humongous van. Imagine driving that behemoth around town with a tiny potion bottle stowed in the back. It's absurd."

Esme scoffed. "Maude parks it outside her shop like a giant billboard."

"Takes up at least two parking spaces," Henny said. "Where does she expect her customers to park if she's hogging all the spots?"

That seemed like bad business to me. "I wonder if that's ever received a violation from Mr. Oliphant?"

Henny perked up at this. "She will once I casually mention it to one of the R.A.T.S."

"Enough about Maude. Let's be off." Esme urged us out of the shop.

As we slid through the door, I glanced at the signage again. "What does Tingle Level Ten mean? You mentioned it when you were talking about Maude's employees, too."

"I'm glad you're already curious," Esme said. "Potion-making is not for the faint of heart. To explain tingle levels, you need to understand how potion-making works. First, there's no special skill to choosing and mixing ingredients."

Henny interjected, "Anyone can toss worm castings with frog bile."

"But it's the tingle that makes the mixture a viable potion." Esme wiggling her fingers through the air. "And that is a skill that must be learned."

I held my hands out, finger stretched wide, looking for any indication that I had even one iota of tingle. "So I can learn?"

"Yes, yes," Henny said. "But with anything, some people are better than others. You can study and train your whole life and never achieve Tingle Level Ten. That's reserved for those at the top of their game. Only

Tingle Level Tens can be called true Potion Masters."

"There's certainly an element of natural ability." Esme patted me on the arm as we walked along the sidewalk. "But it *can* be learned, don't you worry."

Henny wagged a finger. "And don't forget you've got the only Tingle Level Ten Potion Masters within a hundred miles teaching you."

Excitement welled inside me once again. I imagined myself rummaging through the supplies, grabbing this bottle and that vial, cooking them over the fire pit in a gigantic cauldron then wiggling my fingers to *make it work*.

As we continued, we came upon a massive wall set along the sidewalk, nearly the span of a storefront itself and towering just as tall. It appeared to be made of a solid piece of time-worn wood, dark and weathered. Round insets of colorful but cloudy glass the size of dinner plates were arranged in a semi-circle and arched from one end of the wall to the other. They were too high up the wall for me to touch and too opaque to see through, anyway. Deep-set carvings of symbols I didn't recognize ran the length of the wall, too. I ran my hand along the carvings, tracing them with my finger. *They must mean something.*

I only realized I'd stopped when I heard Henny grumble at me to keep up.

"What is that wall back there?" I asked after I caught up.

Esme stutter-stepped. "What wall, dear?"

"The one back there made of wood. It has some strange markings on it."

"Oh, that." Esme pulled in a deep breath. "That's the Chester Hollow portal."

"Portal?"

"It's bad news," Henny nearly barked. "Keep away."

I leaned close to Esme and whispered, "I didn't see anything that opened into a portal. It was just a wall."

"It's all very magical, dear. Best to stay away like Henny said."

"But where does it go?"

Esme paused before answering as if choosing her words carefully. "It leads to the non-magic world. As a rule, no one goes through and no one comes out."

"Why can't anyone come or go?"

"Heavens, dear, you ask a lot of questions, don't you? I guess it's that the two worlds shouldn't co-mingle."

"It's dangerous," Henny said. "Nothing good comes from mixing the two. Stay away and there won't be any problems."

"Are there other portals?" I asked.

"Yes," Esme said. "Here and there. But they're all old and dormant, and that's just fine with me. Ah, here we are."

Esme came to a stop at the mouth of a darkened alley between two establishments, one curiously called the Dreamnasium, where I'd spotted the magnificent dome, its brilliance now hidden from street level.

"Astrid's delivery door is through here," Henny said.

I peered down the alleyway. The tall buildings on either side cast ominous shadows into the deepest recesses of the dead-end corridor. Aside from a large dumpster, I could make out little through the shadows, and the smell reminded me of the eye-watering breath of one of Ms. Ruthie's old beaus. The buzz of unseen flies was the only sound. "Can't we go through the front?"

"Don't be absurd," Henny said. "She'll be expecting these at the back door like always." She hiked the box under her arm and began down the alley. Esme followed and again, I brought up the rear, reluctant despite Henny's assurances.

Esme slowed to my side. "After this, we'll go over the lessons I pulled from the Association's website. They've instructed us to start with basic equipment, then move on to—"

"Oof!" Henny crashed to the ground with a thud. The box slipped from her arm and splintered on the cobbles, shattering the potions in a spray of wood, glass, and glossy green goo.

"Oh my goodness." Esme rushed to her side.

Henny righted herself. Her hair was mussed from the fall and stuck out at all angles, and there was a nasty scrape on her palm. "Must have tripped on something."

At Henny's feet lay a lumpy heap covered in a thin burlap cloth, partially hidden underneath the dumpster.

Esme helped Henny to her feet. "Who would leave their trash on the ground when there's a perfectly good bin right here?"

I bent down to gather the heap to toss it into the dumpster. At first touch, the pile felt squishy. I recoiled on instinct.

"What's wrong?" Henny stepped forward and pulled away the section of burlap cloth exposed underneath the dumpster.

I clasped a hand to my mouth. Peering up at us from beneath the rough cloth was the unblinking, gray-tinged and pointy-nosed face of Chief Rat.

Three

"GADS." HENNY TOSSED the burlap over Oliver's face. "What a wretched sight."

I had never seen a real dead body before. I wasn't sure what I was expecting, but it wasn't the crumpled body of Oliver Oliphant before me. Dead bodies were supposed to lay on their backs, properly aligned, eyes gently closed in the anticipation of a serene and infinite sleep. That was not Oliver. The lump of him was heaped into an unnatural shape, like laundry piled and forgotten on an unused side chair.

Esme had retreated and braced herself against the brick wall of one of the buildings lining the alley. She clutched a hand to her throat. "What in heaven's name… What do we do?"

I exchanged glances with the twins. "We need to call for a constable. This man is dead, and clearly not by accident."

"Absolutely not," Henny said. "Constable Potts is a first-rate nitwit. More trouble than he's worth."

I continued to push. "We need to notify someone.

This is serious."

I could almost see the gears working in Henny's head. "We could leave him. No one saw us here, and it's not like he can be saved. He's already turning into a blueberry."

Esme peeled herself from the far wall. "Carmody's right, we need to tell someone. The constable may not be—"

A *rap rap rap* sounded at the mouth of the alley. Our heads whipped around and framed in the harsh daylight was the unmistakable outline of a uniformed constable tapping his baton against the bricks. His broad shoulders seemed to block the entry into the alley. "The constable may not be what?" he asked.

Esme rushed forward, red-faced and breath heaving. "Thank heavens. We were just about to call for you."

He loomed a head taller than Esme and stared down at her. "What's going on? I hope you and your sister aren't causing more trouble."

Henny jabbed a finger his way. "Don't bring *that* up again. And for the record, I was goaded into that fight."

"What's over there?" He pulled a flashlight from his belt and the beam flared on, trailing from his side to the lump of Oliver at my feet.

Henny took a step back. "We didn't do it."

The constable eyed her sideways as he approached.

Esme wrung her hands. "It's Oliver Oliphant. We found him like this."

He kneeled down beside the heap and pulled away the burlap. I twisted away, not wanting to see Oliver's face again.

Constable Potts rose from his crouch, his face a few

shades whiter than before. "And what exactly were you three doing in this alleyway?"

Esme continued wringing her hands with a look of utter worry on her face. She stood in stark contrast to Henny, who stared at the constable defiantly, arms crossed.

"We were making a delivery," Esme said.

"Where is this delivery?"

"Well it's…"

Henny stomped over to the shattered remnants of the box. "It smashed to bits when I tripped over Chief— When I tripped over Oliphant there."

Constable Potts raised an eyebrow at the splinters. "Mm-hmm."

"We found him like this, sir," I said. "He was hidden under that cloth and it's very dark this deep in the alley."

He spun on me. "And who are you?"

"Carmody Greene, sir."

Esme rushed to my side. "She's our new intern. Started today. Awful way to start, just awful." She gave my shoulders a squeeze.

I tried to reassure her with a weak smile. "I'm okay."

"Course she's okay," Henny said. "Do you think the Meriweather twins would take on a namby-pamby intern? Constitution of an ox, that one."

I stood up a little straighter.

Constable Potts puffed out his chest. "I don't like the look of this. If I remember correctly, you two and Oliver never got along."

"Oliver never got along with anyone," Henny snapped. "Don't you try to pin this on us."

Esme pleaded with him. "We were only trying to

make our delivery to Ms. Starcaller."

"That's right," Henny said. "And if that lump of a man hadn't gotten in my way we'd be on our merry way by now."

The man's eyes narrowed and another pang of fear raced through me. If Henny and Esme were arrested, would I return to Ms. Ruthie? Crazy Barry's?

"Mr. Constable, sir," I said, "as you can see, Mr. Oliphant has already lost a lot of his color. That must mean he's been dead for a while, and we just got here. Look." I pointed to the smashed potion. "It's still runny. We've literally just stumbled upon him."

This caused the constable's eyebrow to raise even higher. "How do you know so much about dead bodies?"

"I… I don't. It makes sense, though, right?"

A wide grin passed over Henny's face. "Makes perfect sense to me."

"Yes," Esme said. "He's quite an unnatural color. I'm sure that takes a bit of time."

With a heaving sigh, the constable stepped aside and made a few calls, then returned to us. "Tell me exactly what happened and maybe then I'll let you go."

After an exhausting recounting and numerous suspicious glances and "mm-hmms" of disbelief, the constable reluctantly released us with a warning not the leave town or cause any trouble. Without any proof that we'd harmed Oliver, there wasn't much he could do, although I could tell the twins were his top suspects, despite the state of Oliver's body.

"Thought he'd never let us go," Henny said as we emerged from the alley into the waning sunlight. "Quick thinking, there, Carmody."

"You really saved us." Esme shook her head. "I thought he was going to arrest us then and there."

"I'm glad he didn't," I said. "But I don't think that's the last we've heard from him. Who would want to kill Mr. Oliphant?"

"A faster answer would be who *wouldn't*." Henny ticked reasons off on her fingers. "Imaginary violations, bloated fines, Schadenfreudeism, and general oafery to name a few."

"I can't think of anyone who liked Mr. Oliphant," Esme said. "Maybe the mayor, but even that's questionable."

"We need a good noggin rustle," Henny said. "Give our old brains a chance to mull it over. I don't know about you, Esme, but I could use a drink. Should we head to our usual spot?"

I looked from Henny to Esme. "What's the usual spot?"

Smiles spread over both their faces and they spoke in unison. "The Drip & Tipple."

* * *

If a dead body wasn't enough excitement for one day, my first steps into the Drip & Tipple surely sent me over the edge.

We had entered through the front. The huge wooden door, carved with a brutish stein clinking cheers with a delicate tea cup, roared open as we made our way inside. What must be the town's most raucous establishment buzzed with patrons, even in the late afternoon hours.

Cheers erupted as we stepped through the door.

Henny ignored them, but Esme craned her neck, looking over the crowds. I took in the place with breathless exhilaration. It was spacious, with a clear line of demarcation down the center of what appeared to be two entirely different establishments.

To one side, deep-toned wooden booths with high, shadowy backs lined the walls. Dark emerald transom windows above each booth let in only an inkling of murky light, and a few tables were scattered about in the hazy film of smoke and dimness that smelled of cigars.

To the other side, the space opened up to a cheery brightness and a faint whiff of floral bouquet wafted under my nose. Rose-themed wallpaper lined the walls, and frilled curtains tied back at the sides with lace allowed the remaining daylight to stream in through large windows.

A steady flock of patrons approached the bar at the back, which also appeared split down the center as a clean marble counter met the dark honey of a wooden bar top.

The Meriweathers quickly made a beeline to a round table smack in the middle of the open room, one side painted white, and the other left as natural oak. A vase of pink flowers sat along the painted line back-to-back with a green glass votive that flickered with the light of a small flame. Light and dark.

The twins took their respective seats, Henny to the darkened side and Esme to the light. I pulled a chair over and sat somewhat in the middle before Henny's booted foot pushed my chair closer to Esme with the wrenching peel of scraping wood.

"Under age," she said.

A moment later, a broad-shouldered woman of substantial height with a black braid as thick as her arm stepped to the table. A thick canvas apron circled her waist, and she smelled like a concentrated mix of all the aromas swirling around the room—tea, coffee, liquor, cigars, roses, and a hint of peppermint. "Afternoon, ladies. Will you be having your usuals?"

"Yes," Esme said. "Jasmine white for me."

"I'd like three fingers today." Henny held up three fingers, spread wide with generous space in between. "Been a rough one."

The sturdy woman grunted, then nodded my way. "Who's this?"

Esme squeezed me into a side hug. "This is our new intern, Carmody Greene. She'll be working with us for a few months."

"What'll you have, intern?"

I'd checked the twins who blinked at me in return. I'd never been in a place like this before. There wasn't even a menu to look at.

"You look confused, dear," Esme said.

"I don't know what to order. Should I get three fingers too?"

Henny blubbered and nearly choked. She turned to the wide-shouldered woman. "Don't you dare bring her that, Roanna. I'll have your hide."

Esme leaned in. "How about a nice gentle tea?"

"Um, that sounds okay. I'm not sure exactly what I…"

Roanna loomed over my shoulder and appraised me for a moment. She leaned down so I could hear over the noise of the tavern. "Neither of those drinks fit you. How about you try my special chai instead?"

"Chai?" I'd never heard of that before. At the

orphanage, we drank only water, with milk some mornings if Ms. Ruthie was in a good mood after having a caller the previous evening.

Roanna nodded and left with a smug grin on her face.

"She won't do you wrong," Henny said over the buzz. "Whatever this chai business is, you'll like it."

With our orders taken, I had a chance to really let the room sink in. There were all sorts lingering about, flowing from dark to light space without a care for the difference. Everyone appeared content, unburdened, even those in the furthest shadows sat in jestful conversation. "What is this place exactly? This is where you go to noggin rustle? How can you think through all this hubbub?"

Henny frowned. "What?"

Esme raised her voice. "She asked how we can drink with all this noise."

"Well, that's a silly question. You just pick up your glass and guzzle it down."

I shook my head and raised my own voice "*Think*. I asked how you can think through all this. What exactly is this place, anyway?"

Without a sound, Roanna sidled up next to me, drinks balanced expertly on a tray. "This is the Drip & Tipple. Tea and booze, coffee or pop. Whatever your taste, you'll find it here." Henny snatched her whiskey off the tray. With deft fingers, Roanna placed a delicate cup of tea by Esme then set a steamy mug in front of me.

Intoxicating spices and sweetness filled my nostrils. I took a sip and savored the spices rolling over my tongue. *What magic is this?*

"Do you like my potion?" Roanna asked me, tossing a wink at the twins.

"It's delicious." I held the mug in my hands, not bothering to set it down between sips.

"Maude was in here yesterday," Roanna said to the twins. "Heard her telling Benoit that you two were selling shoe polish as pimple serum. Thought you'd want to know."

Esme put a hand to her cheek as though bruised by the insult. "We'd never."

Henny's mouth worked into a twist. "That lying bag of wind better watch her back. I've got her number and the next time I see her, I'll show her a thing or three about shoe polish." She checked for other people around us. Apparently satisfied, she turned back to Roanna. "I've got bigger gossip, though. Grab a chair. You'll want to hear this."

Roanna hobbled a chair to our table and eased a long leg over the seat, sitting back to front. She looked from Esme to Henny to me. She must have seen the pallid looks that had taken over our faces. "Spill it."

Esme swallowed hard.

"Chief Rat is dead," Henny said in a low voice. "Found him in the alley next to Astrid's place. Tripped right over him."

Roanna's jaw fell open. "Dead? Chief Rat?"

"It's true," Esme said. "It was awful. Constable Potts is taking care of it right now."

"In the alley?"

Henny nodded. "Foul play, for sure." She grabbed at her ankle and gave it a rub. "Nearly took me with him, too."

Roanna leaned back, grabbing the chairback in front of her so she didn't fall backward and let out a low whistle. "Whoa. You're telling me Chief Rat died in an alleyway. How poetic. Couldn't have happened to a nicer guy."

"Well," Esme said sadly, "I wish someone else had found him."

Roanna tossed her braid over her shoulder, then smacked Esme on the arm. "Buck up. Do you know how many people would have paid to see what you saw today? Chief Rat finally getting his comeuppance. I'm practically oozing with jealousy."

Sipping my chai, I took in this entire exchange. Henny and Esme had warned me that Oliver had many enemies and nearly zero friends, so Roanna's reaction shouldn't have surprised me. But the flippant callousness caught me by surprise. Even dead rats deserved some sympathy.

Roanna leaned in closer. "Who do you think did it?"

"It could have been anyone," Esme said.

"Yeah," Roanna said, "but you've got to have some suspicions. It'll probably take Constable Potts the rest of his career to work it out."

"Alley was deserted, except for the body," Henny said. "Nothing out of the usual. No shadowy sorts lurking about. It really could have been anyone."

"And Constable Potts tried to place the blame on us," Esme said. "As if we'd be capable of something so dastardly."

"Weird thing is," Roanna said, "I walked by that alleyway today and didn't give it a second thought. Chief Rat could have been there the whole time."

I sat up straighter. "When did you go by the alleyway?"

Roanna flinched. "Maybe I shouldn't—"

Breaking glass crashed across the room.

Roanna seemed relieved at the distraction because she bolted up from her chair. "Gotta go clean that up. Enjoy your drinks."

With Roanna gone, we settled in to rustle our noggins. It didn't take long for a long list of suspects to emerge.

Esme jotted down one last name on a scrap of used napkin.

Henny snatched the napkin from her hands. "That's basically the whole town, minus Mrs. Finn's pet goldfish. We've got to narrow it down, otherwise Potts will have it in for us."

"I don't see how," Esme said. "Everyone disliked Oliver."

I pondered this for a moment. If everyone disliked Oliver, then anyone could be the killer—minus Mrs. Finn's pet goldfish. But there had to be a way to differentiate, some way to separate the highly probable from those who were simply possible. "What about people who recently received violations? If we need people who were the angriest or had a motive, those would be our suspects, right?"

Esme and Henny exchanged wide eyes.

"Yes," Esme said. "That's likely the best place to start. Well done, Carmody."

Henny smacked the table with a hoot. "We must be rubbing off on you."

"But how do we find out who received recent violations? Other the ones you got today, of course."

Esme shrugged. "Oliver's notepad?"

"Confiscated by Potts, no doubt." Henny tapped her chin. "R.A.T.S. records would be kept in Town Hall. That'll be our best bet." She checked the clock ticking silently on the wall. "Too late today. We'll have to go tomorrow."

Esme gave Henny a somber look. "Let's hope the mayor has forgiven you."

"I told you," Henny said. "I was *goaded* into that fight."

* * *

We were back at the potion shop and it was late, probably a lot later than most potion-making is done. My first lesson was underway, ready or not, and jitters were getting the better of me.

"All right, my dear, step a little closer." Esme urged me toward the hefty cauldron suspended over the fire pit. Sickly green bubbles gurgled within.

"Don't be such a ninny," Henny said. "You won't fall in."

"The curriculum is quite rigorous," Esme said. "Especially for a novice. I'm not sure what the Association was thinking."

I clutched the carefully measured beaker of distilled water with tensed fingers. Distilled water—that's all they'd let me touch to begin with. Henny had spent a good half an hour ranting that the wholesale prices of toad bile and salamander slime had gone off the charts, and I was promptly forbidden to touch anything without her or Esme's express permission.

"Just pour it in, nice and slow." Esme mimed the

motion with her hand.

Tentatively, I upended the vial over the cauldron and skipped back a step. As the water met the green liquid, the roiling bubbles turned to a violent fizz, and the contents swelled to fill the cauldron. I let out a squeak of terror.

"Calm down." Henny hopped off her stool and peeked into the cauldron. "Not bad. The measurements were just right. That's why it didn't overflow. Always remember to adjust the measurements for the size of the cauldron, otherwise your ratios will be off. Measure twice, pour once."

"Now that you've added the water, let's give it a stir." Esme pulled a large wooden spoon the size of my arm from its hanging spot on the wall. "Three big stirs, clockwise."

I took the spoon with both hands and stepped up to the cauldron once more.

Henny appeared beside me. "Clockwise, mind you."

I nodded, then dipped the spoon into the fizzy liquid and wound it clockwise, using all my strength to fight through the thickness of the potion.

"Feels like stirring hardened concrete, doesn't it?" Henny pulled back one sleeve and flexed her bicep. "You don't get these guns by using automated machinery."

"There are machines that do this?"

"Just take a gander at Elix Mix," she said. "They automate most of the hard work. I bet their potion-makers have the musculature of soggy fish."

"Don't act like we're above all technology, Henny. We have a microwave in the corner." Esme turned to me. "We embrace technology, but some methods are better than others. The right tool for the job is essential in potion-making. Take this simple Tummy Trouble potion. If we were to use machines to stir, it would affect the final thickness. Thickness is important for, um, movement, if you catch my meaning. So, for this potion in particular, stools—er, tools—are important. Cherry wood, to be exact."

I nodded. "Tools affect the outcome of the potion's consistency."

"Not just consistency," Esme said. "A lot of other things, too, but let's not get ahead of ourselves. Why don't we carry on with this potion? It only needs a few minutes more before we can apply the tingle."

"The tingle," I said. "That's the skill that can be learned."

Henny cleared her throat. "To an extent. It'll be good for us to assess your base skill before moving much further into your training. If you're completely devoid of tingle, we'll have to take a different approach."

My heart sank. That sounded an awful lot like a pass or fail assessment. What if I had no natural talent?

"Show me your hands," Henny said.

I held out both hands, palms up. She took them roughly and turned them over to look at both sides.

Esme leaned over and inspected them, too, then beamed up at me.

Henny grunted as though satisfied. "Right. First step is to take your hands and rub them together, as if you're trying to warm them up." She brushed her hands quickly against one another, then held up her palms toward the cauldron.

I mimicked her actions. The warmth of my hands was

pleasant. I just hoped it was enough to tingle.

"Hold them out far, like this." She stretched her hands over the cauldron and twiddled all ten fingers. "Then, give them a little wiggle. Concentrate on the potion, your intent with the potion. Imagine the warmth going from your hands and infusing with the potion."

I wiggled my hands as demonstrated and tried to imagine what warmth infusing with the potion would be like. Was it an invisible tether from my hands? Did it have to flow from my very soul? Perhaps from deep in my—

"You look constipated."

My eyes flew open. I hadn't even realized I'd shut them. "Sorry."

"Try again." Henny turned back to the cauldron.

"You're doing wonderfully, dear," Esme said. "Concentrate on your intention and the warmth from your hands. You'll feel a tug and a tingle in the tips of your fingers."

Focus. I rubbed my hands together and my arms over the cauldron once more. *A tug and a tingle. A tug and a tingle.* The tips of my fingers suddenly felt hot and heavy, as though fevered and swollen from a bite. The feeling was unmistakable. "I think it's happening. My fingers feel strange."

Henny and Esme both leaned forward and inspected my hands and the potion swirling below.

The warm fever turned to fire. "Is it supposed to hurt? Is anything happening?"

The twins frowned.

"Pull her back," Henny said. "Something's wrong."

Esme's gentle arm swept around my waist and she guided me away from the cauldron. My hands fell to my side and the fire quickly subsided. I held them up, sure they would be red and raw and in need of bandages. They appeared unchanged. No burns, no damage at all.

"Are you all right, dear?"

I held my fingers up to them. "What happened? I thought I felt the tingle. It was like a flame in my hands."

"Hmm." Henny mused under a darkened brow. "It's not supposed to hurt." She turned to the cauldron, rubbed her hands together and stretched them over the potion. Her fingers wiggled for a few seconds and the fizzing and burbling from the cauldron came to an abrupt halt.

"Was that it?" I asked. "Was that tingling? It looks so easy."

"Yes." Esme cupped my hands in hers. "But remember, Henny is a trained professional, a potion master of the highest level. You are brand new to this. You can't expect to catch on right away. Why don't we all get some sleep and we'll try again tomorrow."

Henny grumbled. "Tomorrow."

I rubbed at my palms. The pain had faded, but the memory lingered. Despite not tingling, *something* had happened. And in my tenuous situation, something was better than nothing.

Four

THE FOLLOWING MORNING felt like a dream. I was usually a pre-dawn riser, but without the ruckus of a horde of orphans and a litany of chores looming before me, I slept soundly and awoke to the gentle breeze blowing through the window and the morning song of a robin nesting in a nearby tree.

I toppled out of bed and leaned against the windowsill, taking in my newfound freedom. Well, not exactly freedom. I was engaged in a formal internship, after all, but it felt like freedom after so many years at the orphanage.

With a spring in my step, I sailed down the turret stairs to the living room but found it entirely quiet. The twins must have still been asleep. Without much else to do and with a little poking around, I spotted a broom and began sweeping the floors.

Eventually, Esme and Henny shuffled from their own rooms, bleary-eyed and still in their nightgowns.

"Good morning," I said, stowing the broom where I'd found it. "Did you know there's a lovely robin just outside my window?"

Henny grunted in response. "Too early for questions."

"That's lovely, dear. I hope your accommodations were sufficient. I know that room's a bit drafty. It hasn't really been used since…" Esme's voice trailed off, leaving the sentence unfinished.

"It was wonderful. I slept like a baby." I paused a moment. "Although the babies at the orphanage never slept through the night, so I'm not sure where that saying comes from."

Esme and Henny eased themselves into chairs at the dining table and, naturally, I made my way to the kitchen.

"What are you doing?" Henny asked gruffly.

"Making breakfast." I rummaged through the cabinets. "I made breakfast for the other children every day at the orphanage. Usually porridge, but I only see pancake mix here."

Henny stomped into the kitchen and yanked the bag of pancake mix from my hands. "You are not here to make us breakfast. Now, sit yourself down and I'll put the coffee on while Esme makes pancakes."

"We're a bit behind in the curriculum," Esme said. "There's a printout of the next module on the table. Give that a read while you wait. So much to do today. We'll want to get downstairs as soon as possible."

I picked up the module printout. *Potion-making Instruments and Their Proper Storage*. As keen as I was to learn the trade, that sounded about as interesting as a pot of day-old orphanage porridge. "I thought we were going to Town Hall today?"

Esme sighed. "We'll have to fit it in between your

lessons."

"Town Hall first," Henny said. "I want to get my hands on those records and Constable Potts off our back. We'll take the tuk-tuk this time."

With breakfast finished, Esme and Henny led me to a garage off a small courtyard behind the shop. It was just as rough and rickety as my turret room. Rays of morning sun shone through slats of wooden siding as they pulled open the over-sized doors. The hinges creaked and groaned.

"This used to be a carriage house," Esme said. "It's mostly storage now, but the tuk-tuk fits nicely."

A canvas cover lay over a looming shape in the middle of the garage. I would have assumed it was a car except the shape was skinnier and taller than a sedan or even a truck.

Henny motioned for me to grab a corner of the canvas and together we pulled off the cover.

Before me sat a beat-up, rusty, dented vehicle of questionable integrity. Other than a front windshield and roof, it was open to the air on all sides and three small, semi-inflated tires held it upright—one in front and two balancing out the rear. There appeared to be seating for one driver and two more on a narrow, padded bench in what could hardly be called a backseat. A storage rack held on with a length of rough jute perched precariously on the rear bumper. Festive fringe circled the roof like a tacky tourist's sombrero.

Henny slapped the front blue bumper of the tuk-tuk. "Don't worry, she's perfectly seaworthy. Hop in. I'll drive."

I tucked myself in beside Esme on the back bench.

Hopefully, the tight quarters would keep me from sliding out and onto the road on a sharp curve. Something told me Henny wouldn't be the calmest of drivers. Perhaps it was Esme's fierce grip on the handrail attached to the back of the driver's seat before we'd even left the safety of the garage.

"Onwards," Henny announced as she revved the engine. Two sputters later and we were barreling down Main Street at an eye-watering clip. I felt each cobble in the road, and at one point we'd gone airborne before landing roughly on the three strained tires.

Finally, the tuk-tuk screeched to a halt in front of a looming Greek revival building, complete with ornate columns and the chiseled announcement into the façade that we'd reached Town Hall.

Henny popped from the driver's seat and Esme and I slowly lowered ourselves from the tuk-tuk. From the look on Esme's pale face, both our stomachs were in our throats.

"I'm usually the one who drives for deliveries," Esme said. "On account of the delicate potion bottles."

I had taken one step when a mighty belch of blue smoke erupted from the tuk-tuk's tailpipe. I gave Esme a curious look.

"It's a side effect of our Combustion Reduction diesel additive potion. Totally harmless, and you wouldn't want to hear the thing when it's running without."

"Come on, let's see what we can dig up." Henny waved for us to follow her up the broad steps.

We entered through wide double doors that led into an expansive foyer, opened two stories high with a wraparound walkway on the second floor. Light streamed in through high windows and I suddenly felt very small. Henny's boots clomped with every step across the polished stone floor, and even Esme's delicate footfalls echoed throughout the chamber.

Stopping dead center in the room. Henny put her hands on her hips and looked around, consternation clear on her face.

"Where should we start?" Esme asked. "I don't know my way around here."

Henny pointed toward a timid-looking clerk behind the information desk. "You there." She marched forward, and the clerk shrunk away from Henny's aggressive approach. "We're looking for R.A.T.S. records. Where can we find those?"

The clerk gulped. "Rats records?"

"Regulations and Town Standards, dear." Esme eased Henny's bristling figure aside. "We'd like to see the most recent records."

A shadow fell over us and a voice boomed from behind. "Records are closed to inspection."

We spun.

An imposing middle-aged woman, salt and pepper hair perfectly coiffed, in a crisp, tailored tweed suit stood with her arms crossed, looming like a statue. The sun shining through the tall windows dwarfed us in her enormous shadow.

"Theo," Henny said. "What a surprise."

"A surprise to find the mayor in Town Hall?"

"Surprised to find you working."

The stern woman's mouth twitched. "And I'm surprised to find you two here after what happened yesterday. Constable Potts told me everything."

"Everything?" Esme asked nervously.

"That's right." Theo looked down her nose, reminiscent of Oliver's rat stare. "With your family's history, I'm shocked you'd think to dip your toes where they don't belong. I wouldn't want you to get caught doing something untoward, something to besmirch your family name further, if that's even possible."

Henny matched Theo's crossed arms. "Looking at a few records will hardly besmirch the Meriweather name, thank you very much."

I peeked from behind Esme. "Did you say the records are closed to inspection?"

Theo peered behind the twins at me. "They are. Who's this?"

"This is our lovely new intern," Esme said. "She started yesterday, and she's already showing such promise."

That was a stretch, but I appreciated Esme's encouragement.

"Intern, you say?" She appraised me even closer, then stepped forward to shake my hand. "Theodora Papadopoulos. I started as an intern, too. Look at me now, mayor of Chester Hollow. A woman in charge of the success and futures of—"

"Yes, yes," Henny interrupted her. "A woman of vision. A true inspiration. An ego the size of this very building. We know."

"Despite Ms. Meriweather's jests, I fully support this internship. It's good for the town, after all. And I hope I can count on your support at my fundraiser gala tonight." Theo spread her hands wide to emphasize the open chamber. "It will be held right here. This space will be transformed, just wait."

"Unfortunately," Henny said, "I've got a stack of laundry to fold tonight. Priorities, you know."

"The gala sounds lovely," I said. "I'd like to attend."

Henny turned to me, confused. "You would?"

"Yes. I think we all should. I'd hate to miss a fundraiser for such a worthy cause."

Esme turned to Mayor Theo. "What was the cause again?"

"My re-election campaign."

Esme stifled back a gurgle. "Oh."

"Worthy cause?" Henny sputtered. "Not kittens? Not a food drive? Not even a fundraiser for orphans?" Henny waggled a hand in my general direction.

"It's my campaign season, Meriweathers. What do you expect?"

I stepped forward. "As a strong, successful role-model, I support your efforts. We'll be here tonight. Thank you so much for the invitation." I grabbed Henny and Esme by the elbows and guided them out the building's doors and onto the marble steps.

Henny jerked her elbow free. "What was that all about? Role model? You've got to be kidding me."

I put a finger to my lips to quiet her down. "Didn't you hear what the mayor said? The records are closed to inspection."

Esme sighed. "Maybe we could put in a special request? Fill out some paperwork, pay a fee?"

I ducked into a low whisper. "Or we could attend the gala and sneak a peek at those records when no one is looking."

Henny's eyes lit up. "They'll be so busy at their party

no one will be guarding the hen house."

I nodded. "And we foxes can slip right in."

"We'd have to be very careful not to get caught," Esme said. "You heard Theo. She's already got it out for our family."

That's right. Theo had mentioned besmirching the family name even further. "What did she mean by all that? Was it about your bar fight, Henny?"

"Don't worry about that, dear," Esme said. "It's old family business. Very old business indeed. It doesn't help that Henny and Theo have been at odds for decades now."

"It's hard not to be at odds with a woman so foul." Henny glared at Town Hall. "Now I'm in a bad mood. Let's get out of here." She jabbed a thumb sharply toward the tuk-tuk. "Get in."

Esme and I shared the same dire look, then hopped into the backseat of the tuk-tuk with a ruffled and riled Henny at the wheel.

* * *

A little green from the ride home, we entered the potion shop and Esme suddenly stopped. She held her hand up to silence us, then pointed toward the workroom where I'd had my first lesson the night before. A gentle scraping noise emanated from behind the curtain.

Henny's eyes grew dark. "Nuts."

Esme nodded.

We tip-toed toward the back room and once we reached the opening, Henny flung back the curtain.

A small, furry creature darted from one of the shelves, onto a cauldron, over the fire pit, and onto

Esme's workbench clear across the room, leaving a path of upturned boxes and overturned bottles in its wake. A glimpse of fur, a tiny ear, that was all I could make out as it bound around the room.

"What is that?" I asked.

Henny grabbed a large mixing spoon off the wall and held it up like a club. "Get out of here, Nuts, or I'll clock the stuffing right out of you!"

Esme skirted the center fire pit and held her arms out wide, trying to corral the animal into a corner.

For one moment, it stopped, and I caught a good look. *Is that a chipmunk?* No, it seemed scruffier than the ones I'd seen. The tail was a thin, bedraggled mess, and the fur appeared to be multi-colored patches. The ears were different sizes, one with white fur tufting from the top, the other without. He caught sight of me, then bound from Esme's desk onto the spit over the fire pit and up into the wide flue pipe, banging and scraping the whole way up.

Henny threw down the spoon and grabbed a cauldron, then ran to the pit. She held the cauldron over the bottom of the pipe and waited. After a moment, we heard a painful scraping, like nails across a chalkboard, then the animal slid out of the pipe, landed in the cauldron with a thud, and Henny slapped a heavy lid on top. "Gotcha."

Esme picked up a broken bottle off the floor. "He's eaten all the embalmed termites again."

"Darn pest." Henny kicked the metal cauldron. "One of these days I'm going to whack him good."

"Now we're completely out," Esme said. "I don't have another shipment coming in until next month."

I stood frozen in the doorway. "What... What is

that?"

The heavy lid rattled atop the cauldron, but held fast.

"Nuts," Henny said. "The most decrepit, sneaky, spineless creature in the world."

"He belongs to Peter Furlap," Esme said. "The taxidermist."

"Is it… a squirrel?"

Esme gave me a weak smile. "Not exactly. A few years ago, there was a terrible accident."

Henny wagged a finger. "An accident of Furlap's own making, mind you."

Esme continued, "Peter was in the shop showing off his most recent mount, a red squirrel. Henny was ignoring him, of course, and carrying a case of fresh potions through the shop to the tuk-tuk."

"Furlap was yammering on about his stupid squirrel and wasn't looking where he was going."

"It really was an unfortunate accident," Esme said, "but in the collision, an unknown combination of those potions crashed and spilled onto the squirrel."

"Next thing we knew," Henny said, "the unholy thing had sprung back to life, chirping and wobbling all over."

"Apparently, a one-in-a-million mixture of potions reanimated the squirrel. Peter has kept it as a pet ever since, but it's a complete nuisance, as you saw."

"That thing is a zombie squirrel?"

"Yes, dear."

"A *frankensquirrel*," Henny said. "It won't die. Tail rips off? Furlap tacks on a new one. Ear gone? Furlap sews on another. He's been patched up with replacement parts more times that I can count. Theseus' paradoxical squirrel, this one." She tapped the cauldron with her foot again.

"We should return Nuts to Mr. Furlap," Esme said. "Then we can clean up and finally get to Carmody's lessons."

"Yes." Henny rubbed her hands together. "Let's pay Furlap a little visit."

* * *

We made our way to Peter Furlap's shop on foot, leaving the tuk-tuk behind. My stomach was thankful for the respite.

Henny swung the cauldron haphazardly at her side with each stride. A pleased grin spread over her face as we approached a plain wooden door set into the side of a cobbled building far off the main drag. A carved sign hung from a rusty, squeaking hinge above the door.

I read the sign aloud, "Furlap's Fine Taxidermy."

"Furlap's Freakshow," Henny said.

"Let's return Nuts and get back to the shop," Esme said as she turned the doorknob. "We need to get back to Carmody's training, and we're behind on that bulk order of Tummy Trouble."

The shop was dark, lit only by the single north-facing window set into the cobblestone wall. The surrounding buildings cast shadows onto the small side street, only a faint amount of light made its way into the shop. From what I could make out, the shop walls were lined with smaller taxidermy mounts. Rats, mice, and more squirrels frozen in all sorts of creative poses. A ballerina rat wearing a dainty tutu. A mouse relaxing in a miniature wingback chair. Higher on the walls, the heads of deer and boar stared back at me, and birds of prey in full flutter perched on branches attached to their mounting blocks. A fine layer of dust lay over everything like a thin sheet of neglect. The place gave me the creeps.

"No use hiding, Furlap. We've got your little pet right here." Henny swung the cauldron high and plopped it onto a nearby table with a thunk. "Found him rummaging through our stash. *Again*."

A tidy head of close-cropped, thinning hair popped from around a wall near the back of the shop. Furlap's glasses slid down his nose and he propped them back with a bony middle finger. "Meriweathers, what a surprise." His nasally drawl curled around the name.

"We've brought Nuts," Esme said. "I'm sure you've been wondering where he was."

Furlap approached the cauldron slowly, tipped open the lid and pulled Nuts out by the scruff of his neck before placing him on the table. Nuts wobbled, unsteady on his mismatched feet. "My apologies. He has a mind of his own, as you know."

"He literally has no mind," Henny said. "He's a mindless abomination."

Esme wrung her hands. "He is certainly very frisky, but it would be nice if you kept him away from our shop."

"You owe us fifty dollars for the damaged goods." Henny held out her palm toward the man and he recoiled.

"What damaged goods?" he asked.

"The ingredients he *ate*." Henny nearly spat the last word. "That's expensive stuff."

"I can't help it if he's got good taste. Perhaps you should store your supplies more securely."

Henny ground her teeth. "Perhaps you should mount

his squirrely little feet to a cinder block."

Esme let out a squeak. "Perhaps we could all calm down?"

Peter Furlap lay a hand on the table and Nuts scrambled up to his shoulder, perching there like a scurvied parrot. The man's beady, bespectacled eyes swiveled in their sockets, finally landing on me. "Who is this?"

"Our intern," Henny snapped. "Don't change the subject. Back to that payment."

"Intern, you say? This must be the one Constable Potts mentioned."

The constable mentioned me?

"Constable Potts was here?" Esme asked.

He considered Esme before responding. "Yes, earlier. Told me all about Oliver. Sad business. Can't say I'm surprised, though. I've heard this one"—he jabbed a thumb toward Henny—"say numerous times just how much she wished he were dead."

Henny blustered. Her gray hair, already unkempt, seemed to kink at the accusation. "I most certainly had nothing to do with Chief Rat's murder."

He crossed his arms. "So you admit it was murder?"

"Yes, unfortunately," Esme said. "I wish we'd never gone down that alley."

Henny leaned in. "What else did old Potts want with you?"

"Calm yourself, Meriweather. He was just here to remind me about the mayor's gala tonight."

Henny hissed through her teeth. "She's got the fuzz working for her campaign, too. Are you going, then?"

"Of course. I'm not going to miss the event of the year. Mayor Papadopoulos always throws the best parties. Music, canapés, open bar. Maude insisted that we arrive early to solidify our support. It's good business to be seen."

Esme blinked. "You're going with Maude?"

He looked down his nose at her. "Yes. We're what you'd call an *item*."

Henny rolled her eyes in dramatic fashion. "Don't make me wretch up my breakfast."

"I take it you two won't be attending, considering your standing with the mayor?"

"We'll be there." I ran a finger down the feather of a mounted hawk.

Peter turned fully around and stared at me as though I were an intruder. "Is that so? And don't touch that. It's a rare specimen."

"As you said yourself," Esme said, "it's good business."

He narrowed his eyes at me but turned back to the twins. "It may be more interesting to see who doesn't attend. You know, guilty conscience getting the better of them. I doubt Benoit will be there. He never had much respect for the mayor." He let a dramatic pause hang in the room. "Or for Oliver Oliphant."

Henny scoffed. "You think Benoit was responsible for Oliver? He can barely pull himself away from all those animals."

He tilted his head ever so slightly.

"Benoit might just be busy," Esme said. "That doesn't mean he has a guilty conscience. I'm sure his menagerie is a lot of work."

"If you say so."

The door to the shop burst open and a young boy of

about twelve, dirt-brown hair a tousled mess, darted in then slammed the door behind him. "Got the twine you asked for, Mr. Furlap, sir."

The older man hissed, "How many times do I have to tell you not to slam the door, Boyd?"

Boyd froze in his tracks as soon as he spotted three other people in the store. He looked from Henny to Esme and finally to me. His mouth drooped open, and he clutched the roll of twine tightly to his chest. He stared at me without saying a word, eyes wide and unblinking.

"Boyd!"

At Peter's shout, Boyd broke from his trance.

Furlap bobbed his head toward the back. "Put it away then get to work on the Morrison project. Those frogs need to be rehydrated every hour."

Although the fastest path would have taken him right past me, he chose the long way around and had to squeeze past two shelves of mounts and scuttle under a table to reach the back.

"Honestly," Furlap said. "That guttersnipe is more of a nuisance than a help."

"Maybe you should treat him nicer." Esme wrung her hands. "That poor boy deserves some kindness."

"That *poor boy* has been mooching off my kindness for far too long." He nodded my way. "You've got your own mooch now. Come back in a few months and tell me how it's going, eh? Now, I've got a lot of work to do, so if you don't mind…" He held a hand toward the door. "See you at the gala."

As Furlap ushered us out the door, Henny turned back. "Keep that fleabag away from our shop."

"Boyd or the squirrel?" He laughed, then shut the

door in her face.

Five

Henny's mood was pure thunderclouds, so Esme had insisted on driving the tuk-tuk to the gala. Henny wriggled in the backseat next to me, swearing each time the cummerbund chafed under her boobs.

"You could have worn a dress," Esme told her. "They aren't uncomfortable at all."

"Nonsense. I'll take my chest wedgie over that gauzy muumuu you've got on."

"I think you both look wonderful. And thank you for letting me borrow a dress." I stared down at the nebulous form I'd pulled from Esme's closet. Paired with my slouchy socks and clunky footwear, I wasn't much to look at. A cinched belt gave it a bit of shape, but since I had a few inches on Esme, the dress cut at an awkward spot somewhere around mid-shin. But we made it work, and I was grateful we'd found anything for me to wear to my first ever gala.

Town Hall was lit up with a thousand lights, and other guests were arriving along with us. They sparkled and shone and I suddenly felt out of place in my drab dress.

"This is hardly our scene." Esme must have picked up on my nerves. "You'll do fine. Remember, everyone is worried about and focused on themselves."

I appreciated her words, but they didn't quell my anxiety, especially when I reminded myself that attending the gala to investigate was my bright idea.

"Let's get this over with," Henny said. "Try not to make conversation. Mayor Theo needs to notice that we're here, then forget all about us so we can snoop around."

"Right." Esme surveyed the crowd. "Make our appearance then disappear."

I wasn't sure where to start. "Do either of you know where the R.A.T.S. records are kept?"

"Second floor," Henny said. "I overheard Bernard talking about them at the Drip & Tipple once."

"Who's Bernard?" I asked.

"One of the R.A.T.S. clerks," Esme whispered. "He talks too much when he drinks."

"He also gets real handsy." Henny held up a fist. "I left him with a nasty bruise last time."

I had no doubt Henny could leave a bruise with just her glare.

"Oh, goodness." Esme turned and tucked herself into our group, shying away from the crowd. "It's Jasper."

"Don't act like such a ninny," Henny said. "Go talk to him if you're so keen."

I craned my neck over the heads filling the Town Hall foyer. "Who's Jasper?"

Henny waved a hand off to the left. "Tall, scrawny nerd with glasses thicker than Furlap's skull."

I spotted him quickly. Tall scrawny nerds with huge thick glasses stood out in a crowd dressed to the nines. He scanned the group, anxiously running a hand through his thick and unruly salt-and-pepper hair. More salt than pepper, actually. "He's looking for someone."

"He's looking for Esme." Henny gave her sister an exasperated frown. "These two are like tragic school kids fumbling in circles."

Esme had a beau? This was exciting news. I'd imagined the twins holed up in their potion shop wiling away their days in the company of one another, spinsters for life. I'd never guessed that there may be romance in the air for either of them.

Esme pulled her long braid over her shoulder and stroked it with both hands. She stared intently at the floor. "Don't stare at him. He'll see."

"We don't have time for this," Henny said. "Let's get upstairs before—"

"Ahem!"

The entire crowd swiveled toward the sound. The mayor stood at a podium set on the upper stairs of the foyer. Instead of her office attire from earlier, she wore a burgundy velvet gown and sparkling heels. I felt embarrassingly underdressed.

"Hello and welcome. I'm your mayor, Theodora Papadopoulos. Thank you all for coming tonight." She smiled broadly and waited for the meek applause to die down. "Yes, thank you, thank you. Tonight, we celebrate the astounding progress made during the last four years of my administration. It has truly been an honor to serve each and every one of you, and I hope you'll keep our ongoing commitment to meaningful collaboration in mind as we head into this election season."

More weak applause. Apparently, the three of us weren't the only ones attending by obligation.

"As we move forward, it is my promise that Chester Hollow will continue to expand and thrive as the remarkable, unique, and lawful community we know."

"Lawful," Henny said with a scoff. "No mention of Oliver."

Esme nudged her. "Shh."

I scanned the large foyer space. It spanned two stories, open through to the second floor, and a number of hallways and doors spread from the nexus in all directions. From my vantage, I couldn't make out the signs marking directions.

The microphone screeched and Theo tapped it twice. "Please enjoy your evening and spend a moment to peruse the silent auction located in the adjoining room to the left. I'd like to personally thank each and every donor for supporting the right candidate. Your contributions won't be forgotten. And remember, all proceeds go to support me supporting you."

A few claps drifted up from the crowd. The mayor blew vigorous kisses. As she stepped from the dais, she gave the audience a perfect politician's wave.

"Let's go." Henny grabbed my arm and led me and Esme toward the broad staircase leading to the upper floor.

A burgundy figure slipped into our path. "Ladies," the mayor said with slithery enthusiasm. "I am *so* pleased to see you here tonight. Your unwavering support means *so much.*"

I grasped Henny's hand to keep her in line. "Thank

you, madam mayor," I said. "We're happy to be here."

Esme nodded in agreement, smiling so broadly that her eyes squinted shut. "Mm-hmm."

"Glad to hear it." The mayor's eyes darted behind us. "Mr. Lomar, a word…" She slipped away just as quickly as she'd appeared, onto the next target.

Henny squirmed out of my grip.

I checked the crowd to make sure no one was watching, then led the way up the stairwell.

We reached the landing and looked in all directions for a sign.

"Here." Esme motioned to a door a few yards away. "Regulations and Town Standards."

I tried the handle. The door was locked.

"What now?" Esme asked. "I don't know how to pick a lock."

"Ugh." Henny groaned. "Why couldn't Bernard be as loose with this lock as he is with his morals? We should just bust it in. One swift kick is all it needs."

Esme shook her head. "And the whole party will know we're up here."

The buzz of the guests drifted up to the second floor and filled the surrounding air. I slipped a pin from my hair. Despite the brilliant illumination of the party below, the light along the second-floor mezzanine was faint. Bending down closely, I could just make out the lock.

Esme kneeled beside me. "What are you doing?"

I jiggled my pin in the lock mechanism. "Ms. Ruthie always kept a big padlock on the pantry. Claimed we kids would eat her out of house and home if she didn't. But she'd often pass out with one of her beaus before we could serve dinner. Or she'd sleep clear through the morning." One twist, turn, two tugs, push. "I learned to pick that padlock so the little ones could have a hot meal." *Click.* My satisfied smile was the same as those kids' when their tummies were full. I turned the knob, and the door swung open.

"Excellent." Henny strode in and went directly for a large filing cabinet. The placard on the huge desk next to it read, "Oliver Oliphant, Chief Inspector."

Esme shut the door, careful not to make a sound. "We need to be careful. Don't make a mess, Henny."

"Pfft." Henny pulled a folder from the cabinet and slapped it onto Oliver's desk. "These are the records for the past month. Oliver went on that long vacation, remember? Everyone got a nice little rest from his harassment, so I think these would be the most recent."

"Let's see," I said.

Esme pulled the first record from the folder and held it up to the window where light from the streetlamps shone through slats in the vinyl blinds. "This one's ours."

"Rip it up," Henny said.

Instead, Esme set it neatly back into the folder.

We riffled through the records making note of all the violations and the business owners involved. In addition to our own, there were files for a man Esme and Henny called Big Harv, Astrid Starcaller, whose potions we were delivering when we stumbled upon Oliver, Benoit from a place they called the Menagerie, and much to Henny's glee, Elix Mix's Maude and Peter Furlap the taxidermist. The last record we pulled listed Roanna at the Drip & Tipple.

Henny tucked Roanna's record back into the folder. "Roanna can't be responsible."

"Why not?" I asked.

"It's not in her nature," she replied. "We should focus on Furlap and Maude."

Esme piped in, "I don't think Roanna could be responsible for Oliver's death, either."

I'd gathered that Roanna was the twins' friend, but I wasn't so easily dissuaded, especially when it was my internship on the line. "We should keep an open mind and should look into everyone. We need to be thorough."

"I suppose being thorough *is* a good idea," Esme said.

Henny hemmed and hawed but reluctantly agreed. "Fine, but I can tell you now, she didn't do it."

Subtle footfalls outside the office door halted our conversation.

Someone tried the door handle, then a muffled voice said, "In here. This one isn't locked."

"Under the desk," I whispered.

With speed I'd never have suspected of two elderly ladies, we dove under Oliver's oversized desk and crammed into the kneehole just as the door swung open.

I dipped to the floor and peered through the underside at two pairs of feet. One wore sparkling heels. Mayor Theo.

"Why do I need to take it?"

I recognized the man's voice as Constable Potts.

"Because I don't need the scrutiny," Theo said. "Not with this Oliver mess and the campaign in full swing."

The sound of rustling paper made me suspect something had changed hands.

"What am I supposed to do with this?" the constable asked.

"I don't know. Just get rid of it."

My arm slipped. I caught myself, but not before kicking Henny with one of my clunky shoes. She tried to muffle a grunt, but it eked out.

"What was that?" The sparkling shoes turned toward the desk. "I thought I heard something."

"Probably just the party downstairs."

I squeezed my eyes shut. *Please don't look over here.*

We froze in utter silence for a few agonizing moments.

Finally, the heels turned away.

"Let's get out of here," the mayor said. Then her glittering pumps, along with Constable Potts' polished shoes, exited through the door and it closed behind them with a click.

Esme let out a deep breath next to me. In the dim light her face was as red as a beet.

"Were you holding your breath that whole time?" I asked.

She nodded. "I'm a mouth breather."

"She's *very* loud," Henny added. "What do you think was going on with Potts and the mayor?"

"She gave him something," I said. "It sounded like a paper bag."

"Drugs?" Henny suggested.

Esme's hand clutched at her necklace. "I doubt Constable Potts would be involved if it were drugs, don't you think?"

I doubted drugs were the answer, too. Why here? Why now? But, by my own words, we were supposed to be thorough. "Whatever it was, she didn't want to be caught with it."

Henny hastily shoved the loose records back into the folder and jammed it into the filing cabinet. "Of course the mayor's up to no good. No surprise there, but we've got our names. Let's skedaddle. This cummerbund is chaffing my bazoongas again."

Six

THE FOLLOWING MORNING, the twins and I wasted no time in tracking down the recent R.A.T.S. violators. Henny wanted to start with her favorite suspect, Maude.

Esme parked the tuk-tuk neatly into a spot near Elix Mix. A gigantic delivery van took up most of the spots in front of the shop, but it didn't hide the clean, crisp white paint and green and purple neon sign flashing in sharp, modern lettering. Elix Mix was very trendy. It couldn't be more different from the old-world, crumbling brick and moss of the Meriweather Potions building.

Henny squinted up at the sign. "What an eyesore."

The tuk-tuk's rusty joints groaned as Esme stepped off. "What makes us think Maude will answer anything we ask?"

Henny scoffed. "A couple pointed questions and she'll crumple like dried snake skin."

"That reminds me," Esme said, "we should add a package of snake skin onto the order list. We're low on that, too. Oh, my goodness, that list is getting long."

"We can't just walk in and interrogate her," I said.

"We need to be smart about this and make a plan."

Without waiting, Henny pushed through the sleek glass front door. It opened into a bright, high-ceilinged lobby where a spotless display cabinet spanned the length of the room. Two young women in crisp Elix Mix-branded green and purple uniforms worked behind the counter, rushing back and forth putting bottles and pouches into boxes, then sealing each with a shiny Elix Mix sticker. They set their packages onto a tower of similar boxes.

Maude appeared from the back room. Her step faltered when she spotted us. "Meriweathers. What do you want?"

"We have some questions for you," Henny said, puffing out her chest.

Maude blinked. "The illustrious Potion Masters have questions for a lowly potion-maker like me? Get out."

"Not questions about potion-making," Esme said. "About Oliver Oliphant."

"I'm not sure you heard me. The door is right behind you."

"Don't get your girdle in a twist," Henny said. "Our questions are harmless. Besides, don't you want to clear your name?"

The two employees' eyes went wide. I guessed they weren't used to anyone talking to Maude that way.

Maude stepped closer, glaring at Henny. "Clear my name of what?"

Henny stepped even closer, nearly chest-to-chest with Maude. "Of the suspicion that you offed Oliver. You seem to have a strong motive."

I lay my hand on Henny's arm, and she stepped back.

"I don't know what you're talking about. If anyone has a strong motive, it's the two of you. I heard Oliver in your shop that morning. Violations left and right. How many more could you take before your decrepit shop crumbles to the ground?"

Henny's feathers were clearly ruffled. She blustered and puffed. "We've got more business than ever."

"We're doing just fine, thank you, Maude," Esme said sweetly. "We're just taking some extra time to focus on our intern."

"And does she have the tingle?" Maude asked.

"W-well," Esme began with a stammer, "she's defi-nitely getting some strong feelings."

Maude's eyebrows shot up. "Strong feelings, eh? I get strong feelings on my morning walk, but it's not tin-gling."

"Don't you worry about our intern," Henny said. "Why don't you tell us what you know about Oliver. What were your recent violations? We know he was here last week."

"Ha! He was here to pick up an order. I don't suppose he placed an order at your establishment? Seems to be a pattern." Maude waved a hand toward the towering pile of orders. "We can hardly keep up. Maybe if you spent more time on marketing and less time holed up like her-mits, you'd have sales like this, too."

Esme gulped at the sight of the overflowing potion orders. "I'm sure that wasn't the only reason he was here last week. Wasn't there an inspection?"

At this, Maude's eyes narrowed to slits. "What makes you think that?"

"People talk, Maude," Henny said. "You of all

people should know that, so don't act so surprised."

Maude considered this for a moment, then said, "I did have an inspection, but everything was fine."

"Fine, eh?" Henny stepped closer and lowered her voice. "There wasn't a sanitization issue with your four-inch vials? A repeat violation, was it, hmm?"

Maude checked that her two employees were out of earshot, then turned back to us. "How do you know about that?" she asked with a hiss. "No one else was here."

"Like I said, people talk."

"Well, it wasn't *my* people, so who then?"

"Idle town gossip," I said. "This was a repeat violation. Did that cause you any problems? From what I've gathered, Mr. Oliphant didn't like repeat violations."

"Problems?" Maude dismissed the idea with a flick of her wrist. "Nothing I couldn't deal with. But I don't understand why you three care at all. I should tell you to mind your own business."

"Look," Henny said, "we didn't hurt Chief Rat, but someone did. And you seem to have a pretty good motive from my perspective."

I held my tongue, not wanting to remind Henny that Maude's motive was exactly the same motive someone could pin on the twins.

Maude let out a cackle. "You think I killed Oliver? That's impossible. I was busy all day."

"Not too busy to pop into our shop and rile us up," Henny said.

"If you must know, I had an extended meeting with corporate. They're releasing a new line of high-end bath potions. Very chic."

Esme went white. "New line of bath potions? But

we're working on—"

"Shh." Henny nearly went apoplectic quieting her down, but it was too late.

"Working on a line yourself? I hope your branding is on point, because the Rosette Toilette line is going to fly off the shelves."

"How long was this meeting with corporate?" I asked.

Maude paused. "It took all afternoon, actually. The line has a lot of depth. Creams, potions, salves, that sort of thing."

Had she been thinking through her answer? I made a mental note.

Maude continued, "If you're looking for who had reason to get rid of Oliver, just look at the mayor."

"The mayor?" Esme asked. "What's she got to do with it?"

Maude couldn't hide her condescension. "Oliver was going to run against her this year. I thought everyone knew that."

This was clearly news to the twins, because they looked as shocked as I felt.

Crossing her arms, Maude casually leaned back with satisfaction. "You two need to get your heads out of your cauldrons and spend more time in the real world."

* * *

We left Elix Mix in a hurry, Henny leading the way. By the sour look on her face, I could tell the news about Oliver had come as a surprise. Or maybe it was the fact that Maude knew something she had not.

As we bustled down the sidewalk, Esme said, "I had no idea Oliver planned to run for mayor. Did you, Henny?"

Henny's step caught. "I had my suspicions, of course."

Of course.

"Harvey Pyle's next," Henny said. "He was on the list, right?"

I recalled my mental list of violators. "Yep. Violations were 'unsafe and hazardous showroom conditions.'"

Esme ground to a halt. "Now hold on. We need to get back to Carmody's lessons. According to the curriculum, we're behind already. We should be on Module 2.1: Introduction to Equipment Basics and Common Blends. These are important fundamentals."

"Equipment basics and common blends, eh?" Henny turned her sour look toward me. "Use the mid-sized stainless-steel cauldron. It's the best on the market. Always clean your equipment with distilled water and mild dish soap. Never use a metal ladle with a platinum pot. The most common blend is ground marigold seeds and cotton lint. Add that to anything and it gives it a punch." She rounded on Esme. "Lessons done. Now it's time for Big Harv."

Esme gave a weak flap of her arms and sighed, but fell in line with Henny as we trudged onward.

After a few minutes of walking at Henny's brisk pace, she pointed at a sign up ahead. It creaked on rusted metal hinges in the breeze.

"Big Harv's Enchanted Imports & Antiques," she said. "Biggest pile of junk in town."

"Why is it junk?" I asked.

"Because nothing ever works, dear. Harvey Pyle's been known to sell damaged goods. He has a reputation."

"Like a used car salesman," Henny said. "Always slithering around for a sale."

"He must get a lot of violations then," I said.

Henny halted her strides and turned to me. "His place is like a death trap. Don't touch anything. Don't breathe on anything."

This Big Harv sounded like he'd be a tough nut to crack. I wondered if Esme's gentler approach would be more effective than Henny's.

Esme stifled a giggle. "He's also sweet on Henny."

Oh really? I raised an eyebrow at the frizzy-haired twin. That might change things.

Henny rolled her eyes in response. "He just sweet-talks for a sale. He's all sugar, and too much sugar rots your teeth. Everyone, keep your wits about you." She pushed through the door into the showroom.

As soon as I stepped foot inside, I knew exactly what the twins had warned me about. Fiddly trinkets covered every surface, threatening to topple and crash with the slightest breeze. Towers of stacked tables rose toward the high ceiling. Above me, a sinuous line of chairs all connected together along a thick cable hung from the ceiling. I followed the chairs' path as they stretched from the main warehouse showroom beyond a pair of curtains and out of sight like a snake disappearing into its den. Cabinets, banquettes, velvet-upholstered wingback chairs and all manner of antiques in various stages of decay filled the cavernous space. I tucked my arms close at my sides and followed the twins through a makeshift path.

"Where is he?" Henny mumbled. "Up to no good, surely."

Through a break in the clutter, I caught sight of a beefy figure across the warehouse carrying two bulky items on either bulging shoulder. He made it look simple. "I can see why they call him big."

Esme peered at where I was staring, but clicked her tongue. "That's not him."

"It isn't?"

"No," Henny interjected as she pushed past us along the path. "That's Wee Harv."

"*Wee?*"

"Big Harv's son," Esme said. "Doesn't talk much—all muscle, but he's a nice young man."

Wee Harv and his muscles disappeared into a back room, separated from the main shop by a dense black curtain.

"Harvey," Henny shouted into the air. "Where are you hiding?"

From amidst the clusters of furniture, a muffled voice called out. I turned in a circle searching for the noise until an armoire with heavy cast iron hinges began hobbling from side to side on sturdy feet.

"What's that?" Esme asked.

Henny held out a hand to stop us from moving closer. "Don't touch it. Could be dangerous. I've seen these lingering hexes before. Probably an unsuspecting heir selling off the family goods without clearing the residual curses. I bet Big Harv didn't bother to check. He's always cutting corners."

The armoire clanged from foot to foot, and the muffled voice called out again. "Harp mer!"

"Harp mer?" Esme looked from me to Henny. "I don't understand."

"Tur hander." There was no doubt now that the voice came from the armoire.

Bewilderment only grew on Esme's face. "Who's Hander? Maybe we should get Wee Harv."

"Wait," I said. "Listen."

"Harp mer. Tur hander."

I pushed my ear closer. "I think… I think it's asking for help."

"No chance," Henny declared. "We do not help inanimate furniture no matter how sweetly it asks. I'm not falling for that again."

Hander. My eyes fell on the cast iron handle. Despite Henny's protests, I darted forward and turned the handle.

The door flew open, and a lump tumbled out, waving and flailing in a tornado of silks and wool. As the final pieces of clothing flew off, a small man appeared from the melee, his back turned away from us. "Took you long enough, you oaf. I've been trapped in there since breakfast."

"Don't blame us," Henny snapped.

He spun. The sourness in his voice turned to honey. "Oh, Miss Meriweather. I didn't see you there. Thought you were that incomp—eh, thought you were Wee Harv for a second."

Henny's disapproving grunt echoed off the high ceilings.

"What were you doing in there?" Esme asked.

He brushed at his clothes, flicking off a lingering sock, then straightened the thick tie at his skinny neck. "I had it on good authority that this wardrobe had a special compartment that dry-cleaned your clothes."

Esme stuck her head into the open door and peered around. "Does it?"

"Get back, Esme!" Henny snatched her by the arm and pulled her out of the armoire.

"No," he said flatly. "Just a sticky magic handle that locks you in. No matter, there's a market for that, too."

I surmised the man before me was Big Harv, although big was not the best descriptor. Similar to Wee Harv, his name belied the truth. Short with a few stray hairs plastered across his balding head. He wore a suit two sizes too big and a fat tie of garish gold and red diagonal stripes. The distinct feeling of sliminess oozed from the smile. He reached for Henny's hand but she jerked it back.

"Don't touch me," she said with a scowl.

His smile broadened and he winked. "Spicy as always. You know how that riles me up."

Esme stepped between the man and Henny. "Big Harv," she said with her usual sweetness, "we were hoping to ask you a few questions about Oliver."

His smile disappeared. "Oliver?"

"That's right," Henny said. "Big nose. Liked to poke around. Dead."

"I know who you mean." His eyes fell on me. "Who's this?"

"Our intern," the twins said together.

I occupied myself by running a finger through a thick layer of dust coating a chest-high bookcase.

"I just got that in," he said. "Alphabetizes your books for you. I'll give you a knock-out deal for it. Three hundred bucks out the door."

Henny cut him off. "We're not here to buy your dingy wares, Harv. We want to know what went on with you and Oliver before he was killed."

"What went on? Nothing went on. I don't know what you're talking about. I run a successful and entirely up-to-code magical antiques business." He straightened his tie again. "Now, I haven't got much time. New shipment just came in. Wee's already working on it."

"We saw," Henny said. "What are you hiding behind that curtain?"

Big Harv squinted, but it was gone in a second. "Never you mind, my sweet lady Meriweather. I don't ask you what's in your unmarked potion bottles."

Esme let out a scandalized gasp, then said to me, "He's not serious. We'd never leave a potion bottle unmarked. That's dangerous."

I nodded to reassure her I understood, but my thoughts had already slipped back to what Big Harv was hiding behind the curtain. "Business must be good. New inventory means sales, right?"

He peaked a single suspicious eyebrow. "Can't say I'm struggling. That's what happens when you're business-minded. You could take a leaf out of my book if you plan to run a potion shop one day. I'm afraid old Meemaw Meriweather would take a turn or two in her grave if she could see her shop today."

Henny stepped forward. "Don't you dare—"

Esme and I both pulled her back. The gray hairs at her temple had frizzed like an affronted cat.

With Henny stowed safely behind us, Esme said, "We're doing quite well, thank you very much. Now, as I was saying, we wanted to ask you a few questions about

Oliver. Constable Potts seems to think we had something to do with his death, which I'm sure you agree is absolute nonsense."

Big Harv merely blinked.

The pep of confidence dropped from Esme's voice. "We were hoping you could shed some light on any recent interactions."

"What kind of interactions?"

Henny's head craned from over our shoulders. "Don't play coy with us, Harv. We know there was at least one violation against your shop." Her eye scanned the room. "Probably more."

The little man crossed his arms. "Everyone had violations. Why do you care about mine so much? They were just little things, the kind Oliver liked to rub your nose in."

"How bad was he rubbing your nose?" I asked.

"Not *that* bad, if that's what you're asking. He said my shop was unsafe. Look around, everything is perfectly secured."

I did as he suggested, but looking around felt like I'd be smashed by an avalanche of rickety chairs at any moment. Not to mention the magical locking armoire.

Henny broke through our blockade. "How bad did he irritate you?"

"Unlike you, my dear, it'd take more than irritation to goad me into violence. I've got Wee Harv to look after, you know. He depends on me. This whole place." He waved his arms around. "I've got to leave him something. Oliver liked to play death-by-a-thousand-fines, but I was making it work. Still here, still thriving."

The dust sediment and severe lack of patrons

indicated otherwise.

Big Harv's tone dropped low. "You should take a gander at your pal Roanna. Just the other day she was boasting to anyone who would listen that she'd get her revenge on Oliver. If that doesn't sound suspicious, then I don't know what does."

"Rubbish," Henny barked.

Big Harv grinned at Henny. "My sweet, I heard it from her very own lips. 'When I get my hands on that rat, he'll be sorry.' Those were her exact words."

"Utter drivel," Henny barked again. "Pure poppycock."

"Perhaps Roanna speaks too bluntly sometimes," Esme said, "but I hardly think that insinuates guilt."

He waved his hands in dismissal. "Believe what you want, it's no skin off my back. Got any more questions? I need to get back to this." He slapped a hand on the side of the aggressive armoire and it growled back at him.

Henny growled too. "Let's get out of here." She led us furiously from the shop, weaving through the maze with heavy stomps. "I don't need to hear anymore from Big Harv and his carnivorous piles of junk."

* * *

Once we'd closed the door to Big Harv's warehouse behind us, I spun on the ladies. "We should talk to Roanna again."

"Don't be ridiculous," Henny said. "You can't believe a word Big Harv spits out of that slimy mouth of his."

"We need to get back to the shop, anyway," Esme

said. "There's Mrs. Hennesey's order to complete and Carmody needs to finish her current module. We've still got the other modules to get through and we haven't even touched Rudimentary Tinctures and Tonics."

"But what if Big Harv was right?" I asked.

"He's not," Henny said.

I sighed. "Okay, well what if Big Harv starts telling Constable Potts what he suspects? Shouldn't we warn Roanna?"

Henny and Esme shared one look. As twins, they were probably having a telepathic discussion, weighing the pros and cons and next steps. Perhaps even exchanging theories, mulling over the consequences and risks of a—

"I could use a drink, actually," Henny said. "And we can discuss our findings so far."

"I suppose a warm tea wouldn't be amiss."

"Besides," Henny said, "it would be suspicious if we didn't patronize the Drip & Tipple. Might raise some curious eyebrows."

Esme nodded. "The Meriweather sisters always partake in refreshments there."

Two shakes later, we were pushing our way through the door to the Drip & Tipple. When she spotted us, Roanna waved us in, then finished with her customer. We slipped into the chairs at the twins' usual table and a moment later, Roanna set down a tray with a whiskey, tea, and chai. She twirled her own chair over and straddled the seat, its back facing forward.

"What's the gossip today, girls?" she asked. "Anything hot off the press? Mathilda was in here earlier, said there was going to be a hot-air balloon at the town picnic." She grinned like a cat. "A *hot-air balloon*."

None of us were smiling.

"Why the long faces? I thought that news would perk you right up. Well, Henny at least. And maybe you, Carmody?"

"It's not that," I said. "A hot-air balloon sounds absolutely magical." The thought of taking a balloon ride high into the clouds swiftly took over my imagination, but we were here to discuss murder.

"What is it then?"

"It's Big Harv," Henny said with a dour curl to her lip. "He's out to get you. Said you threatened Oliver's life the other day."

Roanna rose to her feet. She was not what one would call a small woman. She was strong, toned, and exuded power. That braid could be considered a deadly weapon. "He said what?"

"Sit down." Henny tugged at her arm. "We're just the messengers."

Roanna plopped back down in the chair, but a dark cast overtook her eyes.

Esme laid a hand on her wrist. "It's okay, Roanna. No one will believe Big Harv. Remember the time he tried to convince everyone in town to buy those knobby burl wood fruit bowls? He said they were enchanted and would multiply whatever food you put in them, but really he'd accidentally ordered a hundred ordinary bowls instead of ten?"

Roanna's eyes darted to the counter where a polished wooden bowl displayed a variety of prepackaged beef jerky. Her jaw tightened.

Henny leaned in. "Everyone knows he's a liar."

"Scoundrel," Roanna said with a sneer. "You know he only orders water when he comes in here? With a slice of lemon. Asks for extra artificial sweeteners. He sits here and makes his own lemonade concoction instead of buying an actual lemonade. But he can say whatever he wants. I was occupied the afternoon Oliver was murdered."

"With what?" I asked.

Roanna said nothing, but by the furtiveness of her eyes, I suspected she was hiding something.

I lowered my voice to a whisper. "If you have an alibi, then why not share it? That way everyone knows it wasn't you, no matter what Big Harv says."

"What I was doing is my business."

I swallowed back the question I was going to ask next: Did she have any proof?

"No need to snap," Esme said with a hint of reproach in her voice, which was about as much force as I'd heard from her so far. "And I think Carmody is right. You should stand up for your innocence."

Esme tipped her tea to take a sip just as the door chime tingled. A ray of afternoon light streamed in, illuminating a figure in silhouette. Tall, skinny. I caught the distinct shape of thick glasses as the figure turned his head, scanning the room. Jasper.

Tea sputtered from Esme's lips and she set her cup down with shaking hands.

"Control yourself," Henny said under her breath.

Roanna eyed Esme with a sly smile, then raised a hand to wave the man over. "Here, Jasper."

Esme reached out to pull down Roanna's arm. "No, don't."

But it was too late. Jasper gave his glasses a quick polish with a hanky from his pocket and shuffled to our table.

"G-good afternoon." He held a felt hat in front of him with both hands, turning it methodically with long fingers. His eyes were sealed on Esme.

She stared at the floor, both hands fiddling with the handle of her teacup. A timid smile touched the corners of her mouth.

"Jasper." Henny's voice was obnoxious and loud. "What a surprise. We're always in about this time. You're always in about this time. Isn't that a strange coincidence, Esme?"

Esme blinked. "What? Um, yes."

"Sorry?" Roanna cupped a hand to her ear, still grinning. "Couldn't quite hear you, Esme."

"I said, uh, yes." The teacup rattled against its saucer.

"Hello, Jasper," I said. "I'm Carmody. I don't think we've met." I held out my hand.

He appeared startled at the sudden appearance of my hand. "W-what?"

"I'm Carmody, the intern."

"Our new intern," Henny said curtly. "Keep up."

He shook my hand, but hardly tore his eyes off Esme.

"W-will you ladies be at the picnic tomorrow?"

"Yeah," Roanna said, eying Esme, "will you be there? What time? Where might someone find you on the Village Green?"

"Um, yes, well, we'll be there, of course." Esme's voice broke, and she took a sip of her tea.

Roanna grinned up at Jasper. "Did you hear there'll be a hot-air balloon? Maybe you'd want to take a ride with our friend Esme here?"

Esme's cup slipped from her fingers and rattled as she corralled it onto its saucer.

Jasper twirled his cap faster, fingers moving deftly over the soft felt rim. "Well, now, that sounds quite interesting. W-would you want to join me, Miss—"

"No," Esme sputtered. "I'd rather not."

Jasper's face melted. "I see, I see. I suppose I should leave you ladies with your drinks. G-good evening." He fled from the table so fast he nearly stumbled.

Roanna shot Esme a look of mortification. "What was that about? Why'd you say no? That was your opportunity right there on a silver platter."

The cup tinkled as Esme turned it on the saucer. The blushing rose of her cheeks had turned a shade of pale green.

Henny scoffed and took a swig of her whiskey. "You forgot Esme's terrified of heights. She can barely live on the second story of the shop. She gets queasy just looking out the window."

Suddenly, Esme's reactions while settling me into the tower room started to make sense. She hadn't wanted to look out the window at the beautiful view. She wanted to get out of there as quick as she could. Poor thing.

Esme stared after Jasper with a look of despair until he disappeared into the recesses of the bar. "It just slipped out, a reflex. I hope he isn't too hurt. Should I apologize? I'm not sure I could find the words. I get all gooey inside."

Henny rolled her eyes. "The two of you are tragedy incarnate. I nearly choked that he had the courage to ask you on a balloon ride, even with Roanna's help."

"That's progress. Maybe in a few years they'll go out

on an actual date." Roanna's chair groaned as she rose. "Gotta get back to work."

So far, I'd remained mostly quiet, but I didn't want Roanna to slip away without divulging her whereabouts during Oliver's murder. "Why don't you want to establish an alibi?"

Roanna frowned down at me. "Like I said, that's my business."

"None of us want Big Harv's rumors to take hold," I said. "You can quash them easily, so why not?"

Henny and Esme, who had been so reluctant to even consider their friend a suspect, didn't come to her defense this time. They waited for her response.

Roanna looked from Henny to Esme and back to me, then let out a sigh and sat back down in her backward chair. "If you must know, I was at the Dreamnasium."

Henny set down her whiskey with a thud. "The Dreamnasium? I thought you said that stuff was a load of hogwash."

"Shh." Roanna peered around to make sure no one was listening. "I don't need the whole town knowing I was there, okay?"

"The Dreamnasium," I repeated. "Isn't that where we were making a delivery when we found Oliver?"

"Yes, dear," Esme said. "Astrid Starcaller is the town's dreamweaver."

"What's a dreamweaver?"

"Dangerous is what they are." Henny wagged a finger my way. "I don't even like making deliveries there. You are, under no uncertain terms, not to go near that Dreamnasium unless one of us is with you, understood?"

I nodded, then leaned in to Roanna. "So, you were

seeing a dreamweaver during the murder?"

"That's right." Roanna's voice was barely a whisper. "And if you're looking for someone to blame, look toward Maude. One week she's in here ranting over Oliver's violation book and the next she was in here with Furlap yapping about how you two"—Esme's and Henny's eyes shot up—"are a pair of murderous old biddies. Obviously, it's a crock of rat stew, but just like how you don't want rumors swirling about me, you should watch out for yourselves. Crock of rat stew or not, people like to talk." With that, Roanna rose and quietly slid behind the bar, immediately chatting up a plump woman who had just taken a seat.

The three of us sat silent for a moment. I wondered how Roanna may have made it from the bar to the alleyway that leads to the Dreamnasium and back again. Despite Henny's explicit warning, we had to confirm Roanna's alibi. We'd have to visit the dreamweaver.

Seven

ESME AND I sat atop stools on either side of her workbench. A tiny jar of clear liquid sat on the table between us. The new day's lesson was underway, and I was eager to start. But first, I had to figure out this tingle thing. The burn from my previous attempt had long since faded, but the memory had not. Esme and Henny made it look so easy. A gentle wiggle of their fingers and…magic. No burning necessary. What was my problem?

"Give me your palms, dear."

I stretched out my hands, palms up. Nothing looked strange or different. No blaring red welts or glittery stars dancing across my fingers.

Esme ran her finger along the edges of my hands. "Do you feel this? Does it hurt?"

"I feel it, but it doesn't hurt."

She nodded. "I want you to concentrate. Close your eyes. You are walking in a beautiful meadow."

The soothing sensation of Esme tracing my hands lulled me into a state of relaxation. I was no longer in the workroom. Gone were the potion bottles and walls of ingredients. I was barefoot stepping through the tall wild-flowers of a secluded meadow at dawn.

"Imagine the sounds around you," Esme said softly. "Crickets, birds, the rustling of the grasses. The coolness of the morning dew between your toes. Now, hold up your hands. Focus on the sound of the cricket. Put your energy into hearing the chirps of the cricket."

Within my imaginary world, I held up my hands, raising them in the workroom as well. I was aware of both worlds, but each were hazy as I straddled between them. Even Esme's voice had gone quieter, as though muffled through cloth. Only the cricket was clear. Its chirping cut through the hazy morning sharper and sharper as I concentrated on its sound alone.

"My voice will fade. Do not be alarmed. You are safe with me. When the cricket becomes the only sound you hear, rub your hands together, then stretch them out and focus your energy through your fingertips. At that moment, you will feel the tingle."

The last of Esme's words had already faded on the meadow breeze. The cricket chirped in my ears, crisp and sharp. I rubbed my palms together to gather a faint warmth, then I stretched them out before me. The tops of the high meadow grasses tickled my arms and hands. I wiggled my fingers, focusing all my energy to the tips, willing them to work their magic. The crickets' chirps had grown so loud I wanted to cover my ears, but I kept my hands outstretched.

The first sensation took me by surprise, a warmth at the very tips of my wiggling fingers. The chirps morphed to a single unending screech. The warmth turned into a burning. I kept my fingers out, focusing. A scalding pain overtook my fingertips. The screeching continued like the blaring of a warning bell. The pain so white hot my entire body would surely melt. I choked back a scream.

"Carmody!"

My eyes blinked open. The soot-stained ceiling of the workroom stared back at me. I was on the floor.

Esme crouched beside me, her face full of worry. "Are you all right, dear?"

Henny was there, too. "Maybe it was the cricket? Should have gone with the bird, Esme. Easier on the senses."

I sat up slowly. "I don't think that was supposed to happen. My hands were burning."

Henny grunted. "Definitely not."

My head was still spinning when the doorbell chimed and a *rap rap rap* sounded from the front of the shop.

A deep grimace overtook Henny's face. "Constable Potts."

They eased me up to a standing position, and we trudged through the curtain separating the shop from the workroom.

But Constable Potts was not alone. Mayor Theo waited beside him. My eyes darted to her shoes as if expecting her to still be wearing the sparkling heels from the gala.

Henny wore a permanent snarl on her lips. "You two, eh?"

Esme, sweet and kind, welcomed them both. "What can we help you with? Perhaps you'd like to try our Baby's Bottom Balm skin-smoothing poultice?"

Mayor Theo scanned her eyes around the room. "No, thank you. We're here on another matter."

"Oh?" The chipperness in Esme's voice cracked.

Hiking up her trousers, Henny brushed past Esme. She gave Constable Potts a once over. "Nothing good, I'd wager."

The mayor narrowed her eyes and took two slow steps spanning the front display case. She plucked a vial of purple liquid from a basket set atop the case, squinted to read the label, then dropped it back into the basket with a glassy clink. "A little birdie shared a nasty rumor that you've been asking lots of questions. Very interesting questions. Questions best left to the authorities." She nodded toward Constable Potts, who smacked the baton over his palm with a slap. "I am aware that you three were found at the scene of Oliver Oliphant's murder and Constable Potts here"—another smack—"seems to find that awfully suspicious. As do I."

Henny opened her mouth to respond, but the mayor continued.

"Now, it wouldn't be acceptable for two—pardon me, three—*murder* suspects to be gallivanting around town intimidating potential witnesses, would it?" She spread her hands wide. "What choice do I have but to come down here and make sure none of those rumors are true?"

Inhaling deeply, Henny opened her mouth. I sensed the volcano about to erupt.

"I assure you those rumors are false," I said. "We've been so engrossed with my training, who would have the time? We've just come from a very intense session and I'm still recovering." I pressed a palm to my chest as though catching my breath.

Theo's eyes narrowed to slits and scanned each of

our faces, waiting for any hint to the contrary of what I'd said. Finally, she broke our gaze. "And what about the upcoming town picnic? As such upstanding citizens, I assume you'll be attending. Wouldn't want anyone to miss it. There'll be a hot-air balloon this year. And don't forget, Chester Hollow depends on a good showing at the silent auction in order to keep things running smoothly."

Henny mumbled, "Keep your pockets lined, you mean."

The mayor's eyes narrowed again. "What was that?"

Henny cleared her throat. "I said, 'We're very keen.'"

She stared Henny down for one long moment. "Excellent. I'll see you there bright and early."

"With bells on," Esme said, followed by an awkwardly forced laugh.

The mayor ushered Constable Potts out of the shop. Henny rushed forward and slammed the door closed. "Rotten apples, both of them." Then she perked up and quickly opened the door, looked around, then shut it again.

"What was that all about?" Esme asked.

"Boyd, that grimy little toad," Henny seethed. "He was snooping at the window. Probably heard that whole conversation. No doubt Furlap will know it all within the hour."

"It shouldn't come as a surprised to him," Esme said. "Roanna said he and Maude were already tossing us to the wolves."

"But now he'll know that Constable Potts and the mayor are also ready to throw us to the wolves."

I let out a defeated sigh. "I think they *are* the

wolves.”

* * *

The tuk-tuk sputtered down the road, bobbing with every cobble and pothole. Esme dodged the largest, but the rickety old vehicle took a beating.

I sat in the backseat with Henny, who droned on about the merits of organic fleabane and the inferiority of Elix Mix's synthetic cleaning potion. I'd already received her lecture on ingredient quality, so I considered this a refresher and barely listened.

The buildings inched by slowly, Esme having the maximum speed of an ancient tortoise, and my eyes wandered as the cool morning air blew across my cheeks.

Ahead, the looming portal wall came into view. From this slightly more distant perspective, the wall appeared even more weathered and ancient, especially flanked by more modern storefronts on either side. The cloudy glass portholes gave off no light, just dull shadows of their true colors like unlit stained-glass.

“Clean-it-Sheen-it.” Henny scoffed. “What a stupid name. I mean, it's entirely redundant. I bet Maude came up with that one herself.”

Her words were background noise as I focused on the intricacies of the portal—the glass, the carvings. I saw no handle or other means to open it.

“Are you even listening to me?”

I jolted from my daydreaming. “Sorry, what?”

Henny frowned. “Never mind.”

“Ah, here we are.” Esme steered the tuk-tuk into one of the parking spots lining the street in front of the

Dreamnasium. It sputtered to a stop and let out a cracking pop as the exhaust pipe settled.

I shimmied out from the back seat. A few yards away was the entrance to the alleyway where we'd discovered Oliver's body. I blinked away the memory of the frozen look on his bloodless face.

"This way, dear." Esme wrapped an arm in mine and pulled me away from the alley.

"I'm okay," I told her.

She patted my arm and gave me a motherly smile. "You'll like Astrid. She's an… interesting woman."

The Dreamnasium lay before us, a sturdy building that seemed as normal as any other, except for the dazzling dome cupping the rooftop. Unlike the glass on the portal wall, its multi-hued hexagonal panels glittered in the sunlight like a shimmering honeycomb.

Henny stepped before me. "There are a few rules. Don't look directly into Astrid's eyes, don't tell her your deepest darkest secrets, and whatever you do, don't let her delve you."

Delve me?

Esme rolled her eyes at her sister. "Don't be so dramatic. Astrid is a perfectly nice woman. We just, uh, don't patronize her establishment."

"Why?" I asked. "Did she *delve* you?"

"Certainly not," Esme said with a sputter. "We have our reasons, trust in that."

Henny grabbed the door handle, but stopped before opening it. "I'm going to give it to you straight, Carmody. Our family has a…problematic history with dreamweavers. Astrid can do all number of mysterious things, and there's no need to give her open access to our minds, which could lead to dark places." She swung open the door. "Let's get this over with."

We stepped into a reception space that was not much larger than would hold the three of us comfortably. No bell or buzzer announced our arrival, but a few moments later, a young woman with long, wavy blond—nearly white—hair appeared through a gauzy curtain.

If she was surprised to see the twins she didn't show it. "Good morning Meriweathers." She smiled at me kindly. "And friend. You don't normally come through the front." Her voice was steady, warm and gentle, like a blanket wrapped around my shoulders on a cold night, and the twinkle in her eye felt kind, somehow knowing.

"Morning, Astrid," Henny said. "This is our new intern, Carmody. Thought we'd bring her around to deliver your order."

"We're so sorry it's late," Esme added. "We had to remake it."

A cloud cast a shadow over the sparkle in Astrid's eye. "I heard about Oliver." Then the twinkle was back. "Perhaps you'd like a tour of the Dreamnasium, Carmody. You must be curious."

I certainly *was* curious, but Henny's warning wafted fresh in my mind.

Henny dumped the potions on the reception counter. "No time, I'm afraid. Carmody's lessons have us all tied up."

Astrid grinned at me as if she could read the interest on my face. "I'm sure there's enough time to take a quick peek. The dome is quite spectacular." She held out her hand and before I knew it, I'd surged past the twins and taken it, and she swept me through the curtain into the depths of the Dreamnasium.

We entered into a cavernous, circular room. Reaching far above me the domed ceiling shimmered like a million stars. It was mesmerizing. I couldn't stop staring at it. Astrid held my hand as if she understood the magic of it all.

Hexagonal panes of colorful glass made up the dome, with some element of swirling stardust similar to images I'd seen of deep space in a magazine discarded by one of Ms. Ruthie's beaus—big puffy clouds of purples, blues, and silvers. I felt small, insignificant, but at the same time joyous and free.

"The Dreamnasium," Astrid announced. "It's beautiful, isn't it?" She held my hand cupped in hers. "Sometimes I stare into it for hours. I find it comforting. Now, tell me about yourself, Carmody."

"Me?" I asked, surprised. Why would she want to know about boring old me when she could fall into the magnificence of the dome? I pulled my gaze away long enough to see her attention was on me, not the ceiling. "Well," I said haltingly, "I came to the Meriweathers a few days ago to start my internship. I'm going to be a potion-maker."

"That's right," Henny announced as she and Esme edged into the domed room, backs tight against the wall. Their eyes flitted around the space, taking it all in with an air of distrust. "She's *our* intern, so don't get any funny ideas, Astrid."

"You must be excited," Astrid said to me. "I can see it in your eyes."

Indeed, she was gazing deeply. Her twinkle stared back at me. Was it that I didn't want to look away from her, or because I couldn't?

"Is dreamweaving something that can be learned like potion making?"

Henny cleared her throat, a clear warning to Astrid.

Astrid shook her head at my question as though she'd heard it many times. "Dreamweaving is an innate gift. It is not something that can be learned, unfortunately. Only those born with the star mark can become dreamweavers."

"What's a star mark?"

She pulled back the sleeve of her billowy linen blouse. About halfway up the underside of her forearm was a birthmark in the precise shape of a five-pointed star. "There are different levels of competency similar to potion-making, but it's based on the clarity of your star mark."

The sharp lines of Astrid's star mark told me she must be an expert dreamweaver the same way the Meriweather twins were expert potion makers. Although I had no star mark, I suddenly wished I did so I could stare into the glorious dome forever. Perhaps the magic of dreamweaving felt glamorous and exciting, and there was a small glimmer of hope that I could see into the stars and into memories, too. I shook the thought away. *Be happy with your lot.* I was going to be a potion maker and would get to work with two Tingle Level Ten Potion Masters. It was an honor.

The remainder of the space was empty except for dark drapery that hung like a collar around the room and a single chaise placed in the middle directly under the dome. Near the chaise was a lone velvet chair, well-worn and inviting.

"Is that where you sit?" I asked.

Astrid nodded. "And my clients lay on the chaise staring into the Dreamnasium dome. It helps to guide them into their deepest memories. Would you like to try?"

"Absolutely not," Henny sputtered from behind us. "Carmody come here right now." She waved her hand to urge me to join her on the edges of the room.

I felt a pang of guilt having disregarded Henny's initial warning and quickly fallen into the intoxicating magic of dreamweaving. I scuttled over to the twins.

Astrid remained calm with a gentle smile on her face, unaffected by the twins' over-protective nature. "Perhaps next time."

Henny corralled me toward the door to the reception, but I stopped and turned back to Astrid. "There is one thing we want to ask before we go."

The dreamweaver spread her hands out as if an open book.

"Oliver's body was found just outside your business in the alleyway. That's awfully close. Did you hear or see anything?"

She sucked in a breath. As much as she thought she could see into my soul, I don't think she was expecting this direct of a question.

Astrid shook her head and her metal earrings caught the light. "I heard nothing. Apparently, Mr. Oliphant was killed sometime in the afternoon, and I was with a client at the time."

"Oh, good." Esme clasped her hands together, pleased with herself. "She was with a client."

She must have thought that would put Roanna in the clear, but I wasn't so sure. "Who was that?"

The twinkle in Astrid's eyes dimmed. "There's a professional expectation of client confidentiality. I'm sorry I can't share more."

"And I'm sure you've shared all of this with Constable Potts," Esme said.

"Of course," Astrid said. "I've shared everything I could with him."

"What's *everything*?" I asked.

"I told him I was with a client and that I heard and saw nothing."

Henny squinted as though trying to squeeze out more information. "Anything else?"

Astrid sighed. "I told him I thought Harvey Pyle had been acting especially disgruntled as of late. I see signs of stress in him, behind his eyes. Something dark and secretive."

"Pfft," Henny said. "That's just Big Harv acting his usual self."

"Were you delving him?" I asked.

Astrid clasped her hands in front of her again. "I wouldn't be able to share that information with you either way. I hope you understand."

I wanted to dive deeper. There was something else I could ask to help us along. "About how long does a session last?"

"That depends."

"On what?"

"It depends on what the client wants. Do they want to glimpse into their future? Perhaps into their past to relive a memory? Or do they want to explore things long forgotten? But my longest sessions are dream delving."

"Dream delving. What is that exactly?"

Esme tugged at my arm. "I don't think we should be talking about these things."

Astrid ignored her. "Dream delving explores a person's last dream, picks it apart from the inside out. That dragon that was chasing you? An anxiety you can't escape. The vast ocean that swallowed you whole? A sense of overwhelm in your love life. The scenarios are all different."

"Was your afternoon session that day a dream delve?"

She stared at me with a gentle smile. I thought she was deciding whether or not to answer, whether it went against her client's confidentiality. She paused, then looked at me with a twinkle again and said, "Perhaps."

"I think we've taken up enough of your time." Esme wrapped her arm in mine and guided me toward reception.

Astrid watched us go, still smiling as we exited the Dreamnasium.

Once out on the street, Henny rounded on me. "I warned you not to look into her eyes."

"Nothing happened," I said.

Henny scoffed. "She nearly bewitched you. Well, at least we cleared Roanna. Not much more to explore down that path."

"She didn't say it was Roanna," I said.

"Who else could it be, dear? It all fits together like a teacup and saucer."

"She also mentioned Big Harv," I said.

"Eh. Big Harv's always stressed," Henny said. "You met him. He's a mess."

But I remained unconvinced. "Astrid seemed to be

able to see deeply into me. Maybe she saw something in Harvey Pyle, too."

Eight

THE VERDANT GRASS of the Village Green stretched before us as Henny screeched the tuk-tuk to a halt along the bustling sidewalk. The motor sputtered, then let out a mighty belch that scattered a nearby crowd. Stark white pavilions dotted the grass and festive bunting hung from tree to tree. Caramel and chocolate notes drifted from a candy-striped tent nearby and the distant plucking of a banjo and chime of a tambourine meant a music stage must be hiding among the throngs of townspeople.

The three of us exited the vehicle. A humble wicker basket hung from Esme's arm, its handle wrapped with a modest bow.

"Is that the raffle donation for today's fundraiser?" I asked.

"You mean Mayor Theo's tithe," Henny said with a grumble.

"We call it our Kinetic Kitchen Kit." Esme lifted one half of the basket's lid and rummaged inside. She pulled out a large round bottle. "Our Lather Lovers Bubble Enhancer. It scrubs things extra clean. Best to follow the instructions, though. The bubbles can have a mind of their own if left unsupervised." She replaced the bottle and pulled out another of much smaller size. "This is our No Knife Strife All-in-one Honing and Sharpening Oil. Just one drop, mind you. And this one"—she tugged out a final bottle—"is our Speedy Spoon Soaking Solution. Dip your utensils in this for one minute and it makes them move faster. Not suitable for knives, especially after using the No Knife Strife."

"I'm sure it will be very popular," I said.

"Of course it will be," Henny said. "Everyone wants a Meriweather basket."

Esme pointed toward a hastily constructed stage further onto the green. "It looks like Theo's about to make a speech."

We nudged our way through the crowd toward the front, stopping a few rows from the stage. Mayor Theo and Constable Potts huddled in one corner of the stage, occasionally glancing out across the faces of the audience. From the abundant turnout I'd have thought the mayor would be in good spirits, but her brow was knit and she whispered under her breath with Constable Potts. Finally, she broke away and made her way to a microphone.

She tapped the mic twice and a screech of feedback caused the crowd to grimace and groan. "Is this thing on? Can you hear me?"

"We can hear your shrieking," Henny shouted, "if that's what you mean." The crowd chuckled but Theo only squinted, searching for the source among the crowd.

"Stop trying to get us in trouble," Esme whispered.

The mayor cleared her throat. "Welcome, welcome, everyone, and thank you all for attending Chester

Hollow's annual picnic. It's always lovely to see your smiling faces and get a moment to connect with each of you. It's times like this that remind us that life is short, so live to the fullest and celebrate the camaraderie shared between you and your neighbors as we gather together today.

"As you know, the village has experienced the recent loss of our beloved Chief Inspector, Oliver Oliphant. While we are all assembled, it seems appropriate to take a moment to celebrate the life of this dedicated public servant. In memoriam, I am pleased to share that the village council has donated this magnificent monument in his name."

Mayor Theo swept an arm to the side, and a circle of the crowd shuffled away from what must have been the magnificent monument.

"What's *that* say?" a man's voice cried from the front of the crowd.

Theo hastily scrambled down the steps off the stage to inspect Oliver's monument. I craned my neck, but other than a fleeting view, I couldn't see much through the other people also trying to get a closer look.

"Who did this?" Theo shouted. "I demand to know who did this."

"Something must be wrong," Esme said.

"Let's find out," I said. The twins followed in my wake as I wove through the crowd, murmuring apologies and "thank you" and "excuse me" until we emerged from the masses encircling the memorial.

In the cleared circle, an unremarkable round stone protruded from the grass. If it hadn't been identified as a monument, I'd have guessed it was like any other rock dotting the green, lying in wait to stub my toe.

Oliver's name and title of "Chief Inspector" had been etched in the stone, but the hubbub had been for another obvious reason: "Inspector" had been gouged with a red line and replaced with the word "Rat."

"Oh dear," Esme murmured.

Henny chortled, catching the ire of Mayor Theo, who turned on us with glaring eyes.

"Was this you, Henrietta Meriweather? Did you do this?"

Henny choked on her laugh. "Don't be ridiculous, Theo. I've only just arrived. Seems you've got some disgruntled citizens on your hands."

Theo rose from her spot by the stone and wagged a finger in our direction. "If you're lying, I'll have your hide."

Henny guffawed. "You won't goad me into grappling with you again, Theo. I won't be fooled twice."

The mayor's jaw clench into a sharp angle, then she waved at Constable Potts in clear direction to take care of the mess on the memorial. She gestured for the onlookers to scatter. "Carry on, everyone. Enjoy your day, enjoy the festivities." She gave us a parting glare, then stormed away.

With Theo gone, Henny turned on her heel, and Esme and I followed suit. She led us toward the enormous white tent that housed a number of vendors.

"Let's get this basket sorted so we can have a look around," said Henny.

"I see Roanna in the corner." Esme pointed to the far back of the expansive tent where Roanna slung mugs and twirled teacups like a pro from behind a makeshift bar.

She wore the same apron I'd seen her wearing at the Drip & Tipple, and her thick braid was wound into a tight bun.

"Don't chip the glass," Roanna snapped at a dour-faced volunteer.

"Busy day?" Henny asked her as we approached.

The growl on Roanna's lips faded when she spotted the three of us. "Glad you could make it, Meriweathers. The crowds are bigger than last year, pushier too. And these volunteers they gave me"—she glanced toward a pimply-faced, rail-thin man fumbling with a stein—"should be nowhere near glassware."

Esme patted the basket looped on her arm. "We've brought our donation."

"Should go for a tidy sum," Roanna said. "Your basket always rakes in the dough."

Henny hiked up her pants. "It'll turn Maude's face plum red at any rate."

While they made small talk, I peered around the tent. Astrid Starcaller sat in the opposite corner at a small round table, deep in conversation with a riveted festival-goer. The woman's palm lay upward in Astrid's grasp, and the dreamweaver ran a finger down its length. She caught my eye for a quick moment and gave me a wink before returning her attention to her client.

Near the entrance, Maude and Furlap scanned the crowd, shoulder to shoulder, with the occasional whisper between them. I wondered what Maude's donation would be. If Henny's opinion held any weight, it wouldn't compare to the Meriweathers' Kinetic Kitchen Kit.

Through the open tent flaps and far off into the expansive space of the green, layers of bright fabric in every color of the rainbow lay sprawled on the ground. A huge wicker basket big enough to hold several people sat upright nearby. Wee Harv, the gigantic son of Big Harv, wielded a mallet, pounding stakes into the ground that surrounded the deflated hot-air balloon. Big Harv, half his son's size, surveyed the work but didn't move to lift a finger.

Another man stood nearby, broad and apple-shaped, wearing a fancy purple suit. A long-haired black cat draped lazily over one of his arms, flicking its tail with each stroke the man gave its fur. The man yelled instructions at Wee Harv while occasionally casting a disparaging glance toward the big man's father.

I was startled from my observations by a shout from Henny.

"Off with you, you mangy scoundrel!" Henny swatted at a figure who scrambled away through the crowd. I glimpsed a raggedy pageboy cap. Boyd.

"Tried to nip a beer earlier," Roanna said with a chuckle. "Little scamp. Reminds me of myself sometimes."

"Check the basket for any nicked items, Esme."

"He hasn't taken anything," Esme said. "He's harmless, surely. No need to be so harsh with him."

Boyd already forgotten, Henny turned back to the makeshift bar. "I'll have my usual."

"Me too," Esme added.

Roanna raised an eyebrow at me. "And will you be having your usual, too?"

A smile spread across my face. *Chai.* "Yes, please."

Drinks in hand, we wandered around the venue, finally landing at the spot where the Elix Mix table had been set up. A tower of neatly stacked round containers made a pyramid atop the table. A sign nearby indicated these were free samples.

"Is this supposed to be impressive?" Henny asked with derision.

Esme eyed the stacked pyramid. "It all looks very orderly, doesn't it?"

I bent down to get a closer look at a label: Hair Apparent. It would certainly catch everyone's eye, and it did, as every attendee grabbed a freebie as they swept by the table.

I slipped a container into my pocket while Henny and Esme weren't looking. Could it hurt to give it a try? I was never one to pass up free things. The opportunity didn't come by often at the orphanage.

An empty table next to the Elix Mix display had a piece of paper with the Meriweather twins' names on it. Esme placed the basket in the middle of the table, alongside a silent auction bid sheet. Next to Maude's tower of freebies, the twins' simple basket appeared particularly unimpressive.

"There." Esme set the pencil down. "That should get them started. I'm sure everything will go smoothly, and we'll get a good price. It's for the town, after all."

Henny scoffed. "Sure it is. Let's head over and check out that balloon."

Before she could take a step, the man in the fancy suit stepped in front of her. The black cat still draped lazily in his arms. It blinked slowly at the goings-on, but otherwise didn't appear to be bothered.

Only up close did I notice the man's suit was a striking purple velvet, its buttons straining around his waist.

A silken cravat was knotted neatly at his throat, and he rested his free hand on the pommel of a wooden cane ornately carved with the caricatures of innumerable creatures—deer, dragonflies, dolphins just to spot a few. In contrast to his extravagant garb, he also wore a backpack with little plastic portholes left, right, and center. From one tiny window, a furry nose peeked out.

"What's that?" I asked, skipping any introductions.

The man's eyebrows shot up, and a sly smile spread across his face. "That is my chinchilla, Mademoiselle Cosette." He said each word with a grand flourish of a French accent. Nodding to the cat in his arms, he added, "And my dear Erebus is desperately trying to nap through this insufferable chaos."

"This is Benoit, Carmody," Esme added. "He runs the animal menagerie in town."

"I cherish each and every creature on this Earth." He nuzzled his nose into Erebus' thick fur. "They are my *raison d'être*, one might say."

"*Every* creature?" Henny asked with a raised brow.

He rolled his eyes in another grand flourish. "That rapscallion Nuts, you mean? He has been scurrying hither and thither all day. Abominable thing—always sniffing and chewing on whatever it can sink its atrocious teeth into." He held up his cane. Multiple bite marks marred the bottom few inches. "An arrant menace."

His words reminded me of Henny's description of Boyd—two undesirables living on the fringes, and in Nuts' case, *not* living.

"Now, did I catch your words correctly, Mesdames Meriweather?" Benoit asked. "Were you headed toward our magnificent flying contraption? Young Monsieur

Pyle has finished preparations under my explicit instruction. I cannot say his father was of much help, but of course he is a known laggard."

I was eager to get a closer look at the balloon and hopefully take a ride, though I didn't want to get my hopes up, so I tamped down my rising excitement.

"I'll just watch from afar," Esme said.

"Don't be such a namby-pamby chicken gizzard, Esme. It's just a balloon—perfectly safe." Henny turned to Benoit. "Lead the way. At least Carmody and I want a ride."

We tromped across the grass toward the billowing rainbow fabric of the hot-air balloon. The panels caught the breeze and wafted upward, filling the balloon to near capacity. I marveled at its size. Surely even this enormous balloon couldn't lift its hefty wicker carriage, especially with people inside.

A grayish-brown blur darted across our path, and both Henny and Benoit let out a curse.

"Unnatural horror," Benoit muttered.

"Poor Nuts." Esme sighed. "We've tried to come up with a cure, but nothing works. Maybe it's time we accept him as part of the town?"

Benoit glowered at this suggestion, and Esme let the topic drop.

As we approached the towering balloon, Benoit used his cane to wave down Wee Harv, who was testing the ropes staked into the grass, tugging on each one to check that it was secure. "We have our first coterie of courageous aviators," Benoit said. "Prepare for our inaugural flight."

My heart leaped as my stomach sank. As exciting as

a balloon ride sounded, the idea was also quite frightening—floating in the air with nothing to break your fall. Perhaps Esme had the right idea by keeping two feet firmly planted on the ground.

"How does one get into this thing?" Henny peered over the edge of the wicker gondola, which was nearly as tall as she was. A steady flame burned high above, filling the taut balloon with hot air.

As if on cue, Wee Harv produced a step stool and helped Henny climb into the basket. I followed, scurrying in behind her, and Benoit joined us with his two animals.

"Cosette and Erebus both love heights," he said. "I simply could not leave them behind."

Esme stared at us from outside the basket, both her hands resting on the side as though unwilling to let us go. "It might be dangerous. Think of how high it will go."

"That's the point, Esme," Henny said. "To go high."

I placed a comforting hand over Esme's. "It'll be okay. I'm scared too, but I'm also excited. Haven't these things been flying for a hundred years?"

"Just be careful and don't let Benoit do anything crazy."

"Well, you're in luck." Henny waved a hand at Cosette's nose poking from Benoit's backpack. "We've got two useless animals to save us if anything goes wrong."

"Don't be flippant," Esme said sadly. "You know I worry."

Benoit stepped closer. "Fear not, for I am a thrice-certified aeronaut with an impeccable safety record."

"Let's get this show going." Henny slapped the edge of the basket. "What's the holdup?"

"A few last-minute assessments." Benoit tugged on

a sandbag tied to the side of the basket. "We are nearly ready to—"

With a loud *thwang*, one of the ropes tying the basket down snapped toward the balloon and whipped by my face. Esme let out a shriek, clutching the edge of the basket as it lifted a few feet off the ground.

Henny stood on her tip-toes and peered over the edge. "Let go, Esme. It's just a short drop."

But the whites of Esme's eyes shone brighter than the puffy clouds above us. Sheer terror. We floated higher. I dared not pry her fingers off, as we were now a good ten feet in the air. The remaining ropes still secured the balloon, though it swung awkwardly from side to side.

"Look there," Benoit shouted, pointing his cane at a small, furry shape scurrying across the grass toward the next rope tiedown.

Henny growled. "If I get my hands on that varmint, he'll get his stuffing extracted!"

But it was too late. Nuts had found the next rope and gnawed through it like butter. The second rope snapped, and the basket flailed wilder, leaning under the weight of Esme clinging to the side. She shrieked again as her tiny feet waved through thin air.

A voice from below cut through the other shouts. "I've g-got you Esme. Jump into my arms. I'll c-catch you."

I leaned over the side of the basket. Jasper stood below Esme, scrambling from side to side as she swayed, his arms stretched wide waiting for her to fall into them.

"Drop now, Esme," I told her. "Jasper will catch you. He's just below."

"I can't," she wailed. "I'm too scared."

"Oh, for Pete's sake," Henny huffed, then slapped Esme's hands. Her fingers slipped away from the edge.

My breath caught as I watched Esme fall, but Jasper was right there, arms open. She landed securely in his grasp, and they tumbled lightly to the ground, both wearing expressions of utter relief.

I cracked a wide grin. "She's safe."

"Great," Henny said. "*Now* can we get this show on the road?"

Benoit had set Erebus onto the basket floor and was now rummaging around, tugging on ropes and heaving on pulleys. The remaining rope ties released, and the balloon rose swiftly into the clear sky. Below, Esme and Jasper grew smaller and smaller as we drifted upward.

"We'll be able to see the whole town from up here." I pointed into the distance. "I can see my tower. And there, that's the Dreamnasium dome."

Henny gripped the edge of the basket and inhaled deeply. "Something about this air… Wish I could bottle and sell it."

Benoit picked up the cat and held him near the edge. "Erebus loves these high altitudes." Then he promptly threw the cat overboard.

A mortified gasp caught in my throat, but not two seconds later, Erebus the cat unfurled a pair of sleek feathered wings like a raven and took flight.

I gaped at the creature. "I thought… What…"

"*Pterailouros*," Benoit said, anticipating my question.

"Terra-what?" Henny gawked at the sleek black figure gliding through the sky.

"Pegacat, if that is more palatable to the tongue. An

exceedingly ancient and rare Greek species of flying fe-line I acquired during a recent sabbatical in Athens."

I could hardly believe my luck. Floating above the town in a hot-air balloon with a rare pegacat circling above me, the orphanage felt like a distant memory. Wind whipped my cheeks like the cool breeze of freedom.

"What a serene experience." Benoit shut his eyes and took a deep breath. "It is glorious to get away from the incessant theatrics below."

Henny side-eyed Benoit. "What did you think of Oliver's monument?"

At the mention of Oliver's name, Benoit's fingers tightened over the pommel of his cane. "That pitiful pebble left for the unsuspecting populace to trip upon? Sounds like exactly what Oliver would have wanted." The sarcasm in his voice was hard to miss.

From Benoit's expression, he didn't seem to be a huge fan of Oliver either—then again, I couldn't think of anyone I'd met so far who had been. Across-the-board, he was disliked by every person in town. I worried we'd never be able to narrow it down.

"Have you talked to Constable Potts already?" I asked.

Before answering, Benoit held one arm straight out over the side of the basket. A few moments later, Erebus swooped down and landed softly on Benoit's sleeve with a gentle flutter of his wings. The pegacat trotted along Benoit's outstretched arm and onto the wicker rim of the gondola. He tucked his feathers tightly against him and they disappeared under his long black fur, then he perched, perfectly balanced, on the basket's edge.

"The constable came by the menagerie," Benoit said.

"Nearly scared my new owlets to death. And I dare say, he wasn't subtle in his inquiries. He certainly has you in his sights."

If Henny was shocked, she didn't show it other than little storm clouds brewing in her eyes.

"What did he say, exactly?" I asked.

"That he found you three hunched over Oliver's corpse in a shadowy alley like a trio of murderous brigands."

I let out an exasperated sigh. "But we'd just found him. Constable Potts makes it sound like we'd laid in wait and ambushed the man."

"Well, you know," Benoit said with a shrug, "inconvenient facts do not fit Constable Potts' and Mayor Theo's desired narrative."

"And what about you?" I watched closely for his reaction. "What were you doing when Oliver was killed?"

Benoit's hand pressed to the cravat at his throat. "Surely you cannot think I am to blame? Besides, I would never befoul my manicure on that vile dastard."

"Of course not," Henny assured him. "Carmody's a curious young woman. She asks a lot of questions." Henny's tone was calm, and a subtle look between us told me she was playing along.

"If you must know, I was at the menagerie all day. A shipment of Downy Puff Owlets had just arrived, and I was tending to their needs. Downy Puffs are very persnickety creatures. Well, Oliver strutted in like a Javanese Golden Peacock with his revolting violation book at the ready."

"Did he write you a violation?" I asked.

"Of course. He always does. Something about animal

droppings." Benoit's fist once again tightened around the pommel of his cane, and his mouth drew tight. His next words came out as a hiss. "I manage a menagerie, what did he expect?"

"So, the violation wasn't anything new?" I pressed.

Benoit's nose twitched. "He graced me with them with the regularity of a fine Swiss watch. I even kept a special fund to pay for them." His eyes lit up for a moment. "Now I can finally afford the deluxe fur fluffer I've had my eye on. Erebus will be thrilled."

"What do you think happened to Oliver then?" Henny asked him.

Now it was Benoit's turn to side-eye Henny. "I suppose the man got on someone's last nerve."

"Did he get on *your* last nerve," I asked.

His eye twitched at me. "The violations I could manage. But Oliver had a… *je ne sais qui* about him. He exuded something repulsive, something repugnant to the senses. He had the audacity to burst into my shop flaunting that notepad bound in Iridescent Ostrich skin. I nearly gagged."

"We saw the leather violation book, too," Henny said. "Waving it around like a trophy."

"But if you are wondering if I somehow took leave of my senses and dispatched Oliver Oliphant, then the answer is no." Benoit's words were pointed and confident. "I may have told him he could take a leisurely stroll into the depths of a manticore's den, but if you are looking for someone to accuse, I would direct you to Monsieur Furlap. I am convinced those two were in league with one another. Where do you think Oliver got that ostrich pelt in the first place? Peter had it trussed up in his begrimed window like a prized boar."

I struggled to make the connection Benoit was suggesting. "What makes you think Mr. Furlap would have done it? Just because Oliver bought something from him?"

Benoit looked at me aghast. "Anyone capable of such abominable treatment toward another living creature could be capable of *anything*. Just look at that Frankensquirrel, Nuts."

The various derisive comments Benoit had made toward Nuts ran through my mind, but I dared not remind him. I supposed Nuts wasn't technically considered a living creature, but I still felt a little sorry for him, despite him chewing on the balloon ropes *and* breaking into the shop and eating all the Meriweather's embalmed termites.

Maybe we were on the wrong track with Oliver. Violations seemed to be a daily trend, but Benoit had brought up another possibility. What if it wasn't Oliver's work as Chief Rat that had been his downfall but an entirely different angle? And Furlap was a great place to start.

Nine

THE NEXT DAY, we were back in the shop, running through outstanding orders and reviewing inventory. Henny and Esme flitted around the workroom, meticulously ticking off each item and the current status of their orders. Despite a decent night of sleep, my eyes drooped.

"Pay attention, dear," Esme said to me. "The business side of a potion shop may not be exciting, but it's terribly important."

I perked upright and feigned interest.

Esme tapped a line on her clipboard. "We've got to prepare Jody Halverson's leave potion."

"What's a leave potion?" I asked.

"Have you ever heard of a love potion?" Henny asked.

I nodded.

"Well, this is the exact opposite. It's for when you don't want someone to fall in love with you, or when you want to chase someone away. Jody's got an admirer she wants off her tail."

"Can you make love potions?" I asked.

Esme let out a chuckle. "A love potion would be the Holy Grail of potion-making—well, aside from turning trash into gold. That's dangerous stuff, though, and we don't dabble in dangerous potion-making. There are strict Association guidelines against it." Esme gave a clipped nod as if that was all that needed to be said on the matter.

Henny rustled through a stack of papers next to the register. "Have you seen the invoice for Mrs. Chiang? I could have sworn I left it right here."

"Right there?" Esme eyed a disordered stack of loose papers. "I have no possible idea how it could have gotten lost."

Papers were tossed left and right as Henny dug into the pile. "There's a method to my record-keeping."

"Your method doesn't seem to be working; otherwise, you wouldn't be asking me about that invoice."

That roused me from my boredom. "Maybe that's something I could help with? I used to help Ms. Ruthie with all her record-keeping at the orphanage."

Henny grumbled. "I bet you did, and I bet you did most of everything."

"Ms. Ruthie said it would build my character to manage the paperwork."

Esme shook her head and tutted. "I'm starting to think Ms. Ruthie wasn't a virtuous woman. But you're not here to organize our paperwork, Carmody. We should get to your next lesson. I believe the curriculum indicates we should be at *Beginner Salves and Serum Theorems*."

"Jody's leave potion is a beginner-level serum," Henny said. "She can prepare that."

"Do you think I'm ready?" I asked. "What about that pain in my fingers?"

"Probably just a side effect," Henny said. "I wouldn't worry about it. When I first started making potions, my hair would frizz out like I'd been electrocuted. It all calmed down eventually."

I didn't have the heart to tell her it still looked that way.

A shadow passed by the front windows, catching our attention. Constable Potts. I felt the mood in the room darken, and we stiffened, hoping he wouldn't come through the door. He walked on, and we all let out the breath we'd been holding.

"I'm glad he didn't come in here," Esme said. "I'm not sure I could face another round of accusations."

I felt the same way. "We should run through our suspect list again."

"Right." Henny slapped her hands onto her hips. "Who's first?"

"I think Mayor Theo has a lot to answer for," Esme said. "Oliver was going to run against her in the election, after all."

"Would he have any chance of winning, though?" Henny asked. "Between the two of them, I'd rather vote for Nuts."

"He could have been a barrier to her winning easily," I said.

"She's never had anyone run against her before. It's always been smooth sailing." Henny glided her hand through the air. "Nary a ripple in her sail."

"And she was acting strangely at the gala," Esme added. "Remember what we overheard in Oliver's office?"

Henny tapped her chin. "That exchange with Potts

was suspicious, but backroom dealings are nothing new for the mayor. We were just strong-armed into attending the gala and threatened into that picnic fundraiser. It comes so naturally to her."

"Definitely hiding something," I said.

"Then there's Furlap." Henny's tone was as bitter as pith. "The man's a walking red flag. Probably dealing in illegal pelt trading."

Esme scribbled a note on her inventory checklist then replaced a jar of pickled pill bugs on the shelf with a heavy sigh. "But what does any of that have to do with Oliver's death?"

Henny bristled. "I'm sure the connection's there. We just need to suss it out."

"Who else, other than Furlap and Mayor Theo?" I asked.

"Maude the Fraud, of course," Henny said. "If she's been trying to pin the murder on us, maybe she was looking for—or creating—the opportunity to get rid of us."

Maude was certainly on my mind, and I didn't like that she was spreading rumors about the twins. But was she capable of murder just to rid herself of a rival?

A crease of worry shadowed Esme's face. "Maude makes me uncomfortable. I don't know what she's capable of, but I've never seen her use violence. And how would she overpower Oliver, anyway? He's twice as tall as her."

Henny waved her off. "I'm sure she'd find a way—maybe with those uniformed minions of hers."

"Are we the ones spreading rumors now?" Esme asked. "Jumping to conclusions? We're as bad as Maude."

"What about Astrid?" I asked. "She had violations, too."

The Dreamnasium coalesced in my mind—the cool, calm, and collected way Astrid guided me into that space and enchanted me with its possibilities. I shivered.

"Roanna was with her," Henny argued, "so Astrid can't be the killer."

"You're jumping to more conclusions," I said. "We only have the two of them as each other's alibi."

Esme tutted. "Listen to us. Talking about alibis and murder. I don't like any of it. We're supposed to be protecting Carmody from this type of thing."

"I'm all right," I said. "I've read lots of gory headlines in newspapers and magazines. I've even watched crime shows when Ms. Ruthie would let us watch television."

"Well," Esme said, "I for one don't like all the negativity. You're behind on the curriculum, and the Association is going to check on us at any time to ensure your progress."

Progress would be meaningless if the twins were arrested for murder. "Then I'll study extra hard," I said. "Once we put this murder business behind us, there'll be more time. Who's left?"

"Big Harv." Henny nearly spat out the name.

Esme nodded vigorously. "He was definitely hiding something in that warehouse."

"That man's always up to something."

"Then there's Benoit," Esme said. "He may have given you two information about that horrible pelt, but don't forget he had violations of his own."

The image of Benoit's fingers steeling around the

pommel of his cane at the mention of Oliver popped into my head.

"I doubt there's anyone who loves animals more than Benoit," I said. "I can only imagine how Oliver flaunting his elaborate notebook cover would've gone over. Even his dislike of Nuts is rooted in a love of animals. Nuts should have been allowed to rest in peace."

Henny tapped her chin again. "I agree, Benoit is definitely on the list."

"There's someone we're forgetting," I said. "Ro-anna."

"I thought we'd agreed that she and Astrid weren't suspects anymore," Henny said.

"I'm not willing to cut them out completely."

"Waste of time if you ask me," Henny responded quickly. "We should focus on Furlap and Maude. Maybe both of them together. They're the lowest of the low, other than that rat Oliver, of course."

The doorbell jingled, and a gust of wind swept into the shop. We hurried to the front. A woman wearing winter mittens and an oversized coat, the hood draped heavily over her head, bustled in and rushed to the counter.

"Evelyn?" Esme asked. "Is that you? Why are you all bundled up in May?"

"Yes, it's me," the woman whispered. "I need your help."

"What's wrong?" Esme asked.

The woman grabbed the edge of her hood and slowly pulled it back, revealing a dramatic mane of long brown hair like an overgrown mohawk cascading down her back. Thick, glossy strands hung nearly to the floor.

"Oh dear."

"What the heck happened to you?" Henny blurted out. "You look like a horse."

The woman tucked her hair in and shoved the hood back over her head. "That's why I'm here! I tried Maude's salve—the free one she was handing out at the fundraiser yesterday—and then I woke up with *this*. I tried cutting it off, but it grew back in seconds. Even my fingers grew hair. Anything that touched that stuff."

My eyes bulged, remembering the salve I'd pocketed at the event. It remained untouched, thankfully.

The smugness on Henny's face could not be hidden. "Guess that's what you get from Maude and her dodgy quality products."

"I don't need a lecture," Evelyn snapped. "I need a solution. Can you help me or not? The nearest magical salon is nearly three hours away."

Henny hiked up her pants. "We'll see what we can put together."

"Why don't you have a seat?" Esme gestured to a threadbare bench near the door. "We'll get you all sorted out."

We headed to the backroom, Henny and Esme's heads already together.

"What about a shortening potion?" Henny asked.

Esme nodded, deep in thought. "What if we mixed a shortening potion with a stop potion? That would take care of both her issues."

I listened intently as the two went back and forth, running through a slew of possibilities. This was more ed-ucation than I'd get from that dreary curriculum the As-sociation had put together.

"Oh dear." Esme's shoulder drooped. "We can't do

a shortening potion. We're out of salamander slime and it's on backorder, remember? Besides, Nuts ate all of our embalmed termites."

Henny growled under her breath at the mention of Nuts. "We could substitute with blue cornflower petals. It might not be quite as effective, but it'll work."

"Yes, yes," Esme nodded. "That should do nicely. Come along, Carmody. This recipe should be simple enough and it will be an excellent teaching moment."

"And whatever we come up with," Henny added, practically cackling with joy, "we can bottle it, slap a label on it, and sell it to all those fools who picked up Maude's freebie."

A sting of shame rippled through me as I thought about the salve on my nightstand, just waiting to send me into a spiral of embarrassment. I should never have accepted anything from the twins' rival.

Solution decided, Henny and Esme split up, each gathering various accouterments for the potion.

"Carmody, dear," Esme called, "could you grab the twelve-inch cauldron and the largest rowan wood mixing spoon?"

I rummaged through the stack, eventually finding the correct-sized stainless-steel cauldron buried beneath a pile of copper mixing bowls. Next, I went to the spoon wall and ran my fingers along the row markers until I found the right one.

We met at the fire pit in the middle of the room—Esme with an armful of ingredients, Henny clutching a hastily scribbled recipe, and me bearing the cauldron and spoon.

Esme bent down and lit the kindling. "Set the

cauldron in the center, and we'll get the fire going."

"From my estimation," Henny said, squinting at the recipe, "we'll want a gallon of distilled water and we'll need to double the cornflower petals. Then, stir counterclockwise at a slow churn for fifteen seconds, add three tablespoons of powdered hen-of-the-woods, and stir clockwise for another fifteen seconds at a normal pace."

"That sounds simple enough." Esme turned to me. "Do you think this is something you want to try?"

Henny grunted. "She's got to get that tingle sorted out. This would be a good test, no doubt."

My chest tightened as I thought about the times I'd been asked to tingle, only to be left with the burning sensation in my fingers. Would this time be any different?

"Step up, my dear," Esme encouraged. "A little closer."

I inched toward the cauldron, clutching the rowan wood spoon like a vise. Esme poured the cornflower petals into the vessel, along with a gallon of distilled water Henny had measured out.

"There you go," Esme said, placing a comforting hand on my back. "Give it fifteen seconds counterclockwise nice and slow. We'll count for you and let you know when to switch directions."

I nodded, hearing her words but barely processing them. My thoughts were consumed by the burn I feared would come.

Spoon in hand, I began stirring dutifully, and when the time came, Henny added the hen-of-the-woods mushroom powder. Another fifteen seconds passed. The moment had come.

"All done with the mix," Henny said. "Carmody, put

your hands out." She handed the spoon to Esme and turned back to me. "Now, get ready."

Esme added, "Remember the crickets, dear. Think of the crickets."

"Birds," Henny corrected. "Think of birds. Crickets are too loud, too chirpy."

"Birds are chirpy too," Esme muttered under her breath.

Crickets, birds—it didn't matter. I knew what would happen. I cleared my mind, rubbed my hands together, then stretched them out over the cauldron, visualizing the tips of my fingers and imagining a gentle tingle emanating from them like the warmth from a mug of tea or the comforting heat from the fur of a kitten.

I wiggled my fingers.

"Wiggle harder," Henny instructed. "It's like you're in slow motion."

"Let her get there on her own terms," Esme said gently. "You're doing fine, dear."

Then it started. First, a warmth growing slowly at the tips of my fingers. Determined to get it right this time, I pushed through, even as the heat intensified. There was no scar or redness after the previous times, so there wouldn't be this time either. I just had to persevere.

Despite the pain, I focused harder. I thought of the orphanage—my small room shared with eight other girls, the meager meals, the endless hours of chores, Ms. Ruthie's stern discipline. No, I wouldn't go back.

I embraced the burn, focusing entirely on the sensation. In some ways, it disappeared, became a numbness. My fingers seemed to move on their own. I watched them wriggle over the concoction as though observing from outside my own body. My heart leaped—something was happening.

A bright, silent flash of light burst through the work-room.

Instinctively, I jerked my hands back to cover my eyes just as Henny and Esme did the same.

"Good heavens!" Esme exclaimed. "What was that?"

"No idea," Henny replied, steadying herself. She peered into the cauldron, her face a mask of disbelief.

"What?" Esme asked, scrambling to the cauldron herself.

They both turned to me, slack-jawed.

"What happened?" I asked. "Did I tingle? I felt something. What was that light?"

"It's…" Esme voice trailed off. "It's perfection."

Henny eyed me sideways. "Not sure what just happened, but the potion is complete." She gazed into the cauldron again. "Not just complete, it's potent and pure. Let's bottle it up."

Esme nodded, still looking uncertain.

I was confused, too. Whenever Henny or Esme tingled, there was no bright flash of light. But whatever had happened, it seemed to have worked. *Perfection* Esme had called it, and Henny was already ladling the mixture into tiny jars.

"Esme, give this to Evelyn. Tell her we'll send her an invoice. Ten dollars or something. Just get her on her way."

Esme scurried to the front of the shop while Henny turned back to me. She grabbed my hands, inspecting them closely.

"No markings." She turned my hands over. "Can't

say it isn't odd, but I do believe you just tingled for the very first time."

Did I hear her right? Did she say I tingled? A broad smile spread across my face. Pain or not, I was going to be a potion maker.

* * *

Later that day, Henny and Esme bustled me out of the potion shop and into the tuk-tuk. In my arms was a basket full of small containers, each filled with the potion I had just made. Pride radiated from my whole being. My first potion, my first success in the workshop, and it was already going out to customers.

"We need to get these out fast while the market's hot," Henny said, her tone brisk. "They'll be snatched up left and right." She tossed a thumb toward the rack bolted to the tuk-tuk. "Chuck those in the back, Carmody. Let's get on the road. I'm sure at least a hundred people picked up Maude's freebies."

Henny made for the driver's seat, but Esme caught her by the shoulder. "Perhaps I should drive, considering our precious cargo might break under, let's say, more *strenuous* driving." She raised an eyebrow.

Henny frowned, grumbling under her breath, but climbed into the backseat beside me.

"We should start with Furlap," I said. "After what Benoit told us, we'll want to talk to him, anyway. And since he's close with Maude, I'm sure he picked up one of the samples."

"Good idea." Henny's eyes gleamed. "Let's put Furlap in the hot seat."

Esme glided the tuk-tuk to a stop outside Furlap's Fine Taxidermy. The sign above the door creaked in the wind. If I hadn't been there before and knew what to expect, I'd have thought the place was deserted.

Henny barged through the door, her shoes clomping against the wooden floor, announcing her arrival.

Boyd stood in a corner, sweeping. His eyes bulged when he saw us and, without a word, he scurried to the backroom, disappearing from sight.

Moments later, Nuts appeared from one of the shelves lining the walls. He jumped to the table in the middle of the room, sniffed the air, then scampered after Boyd.

A beat passed, and Peter Furlap emerged from behind a curtain, an oversized top hat perched on his head like a cockscomb. His expression was sour.

"What is it now?" he asked, his voice sharp. "I'm sure you're not here to make a purchase."

"Interesting hat," Henny said, clearly amused. "Can't say I often see you patronizing the haberdasher."

Furlap's eyes narrowed. "Since when are you so interested in my wardrobe?"

While Henny and Furlap traded barbs, I wandered along the edge of the room, inspecting the taxidermy mounts again. They were eerily lifelike, and I couldn't help but marvel at the craftsmanship.

It wasn't long before I felt a presence trailing me. A quick glance over my shoulder revealed Boyd's blotchy, dirt-streaked face. His eyes darted away as soon as he realized I'd spotted him. *Had Furlap sent him to follow me?*

I continued my perusal of Furlap's past projects. Some were for sale, with aged price tags dangling from worn strings: fifty dollars, one hundred dollars. The prices seemed reasonable for the craftsmanship, though I wasn't exactly well-versed in retail pricing. Not that it mattered—I had no money. Not that I'd want a—

I turned and grabbed a small standing mount of a mouse from one shelf, flipping the price tag. *At least not for forty bucks.*

Peeking over my shoulder, I checked on Boyd. He lurked a few feet behind me, silently keeping pace as I meandered through the shelves.

I came to a wall adorned with mounts covering the entire space. The nearest was a small, iridescent fish captured mid-thrash, as though it were swimming up a gentle brook.

Behind me, Henny and Furlap continued their exchange. If this kept up, we'd get nowhere. I decided to intervene "Mr. Furlap, where do you get your subjects?" I asked, pointing toward the struggling fish.

Furlap straightened up at the question, tugging at his vest to compose himself. "Oh, here and there. Mostly, people want their big fish mounted. Though, truth be told, I rarely see *big* fish. Mostly minnows and juvenile trout—nothing to write home about. But my patrons often think they've caught 'the big one' and want it displayed."

"So these aren't all your own specimens?" I pressed.

"Some are," he replied. "Mostly, I purchase them from others who would otherwise dispose of them. I give them new life by capturing them in their most natural habitat."

I glanced again at the fish, picturing it struggling up the imagined stream.

"Those fish are the worst to work on—stinky things,"

Furlap said, curling his nose. "You've got to work quickly."

"Ever get a violation for stinky fish?" Henny asked, smirking.

Furlap pursed his lips. "Once or twice, but it wasn't anything serious."

"What about rare animals?" I asked. "Do you ever get those?"

The taxidermist blinked, his expression shifting. "Rare animals?" he repeated. "Working on rare or exotic animals requires a special permit. Quite expensive, and I'm a very frugal businessman."

"You're a skinflint," Henny quipped.

He shot her a glare. "An odd choice of words. But yes, and there's a lot of extra paperwork."

"How about an Iridescent Ostrich pelt for Oliver?" I asked.

His eyes narrowed. "Doesn't ring a bell."

"Benoit seems to think you've had dealings with that pelt," Henny said.

"Benoit always thinks I'm up to no good. He hates my work, harasses me, calls me names, tries to ruin my business. What if I told you I saw a shady individual who looked just like Benoit meeting with Oliver the day of his murder?"

I froze at this new information.

"A shady individual?" Esme repeated, her voice quavering. "Benoit?"

"He wore a long trench coat and dark hat—couldn't see much of him. That's why he was shady, trying to hide who he was. But he was tall and rotund, just like Benoit."

"You're making this up because Benoit accused you

of something," Henny said sharply. "How could you know if this person looked just like Benoit if you said yourself he was hard to see?"

"I don't care if you believe me or not," Furlap said, his tone dismissive. He motioned to the door with an aggressive flourish of his hand, but as he did, his top hat tumbled to the floor, revealing a magnificent mane of long, flowing hair. He scrambled to hide it, sweeping it back up under the brim, but it was too late.

"Ho ho," Henny chuckled. "Looks like you've been partaking in Maude's dodgy salve, too. Well, it's your lucky day." She pulled a tiny bottle from her bag. "We just happen to have the antidote to your troubles. And it can be yours for a couple hundred bucks."

Esme stammered, "But we only charged Evelyn—"

Henny cut her off. "Proven solution. Two hundred bucks and it's yours."

Furlap balked. "A ridiculous price for such a tiny jar."

"All right." Henny moved slowly to tuck the bottle back into her bag. "I suppose you could go to Maude for a fix. Just hope she doesn't make that mane of yours ten times longer. Her potions tend to have side effects. But you already know that, don't you?"

"I'll give you a hundred," Furlap said.

"One fifty. *And* we have more questions we want answered."

His jaw clenched as he considered. "Fine. But it had better work, or I'll take my case to Town Hall. I'm sure Mayor Theo would love to hear about your strong-arm tactics."

"I bet she would," Henny said. "Probably steal a few

of our *strong-arm tactics* for herself. But that won't be necessary. This recipe is one-hundred percent guaranteed."

Furlap disappeared into the back of his shop and reappeared with a few crisp bills. Henny snatched them from his hands and passed the money to Esme, who stared at it wide-eyed like ill-gotten contraband before stuffing it into a pocket out of sight. Henny dropped a tiny jar of my potion into Furlap's desperate hand.

With the deal done, I pressed further. "Tell us what you saw in the alleyway. Benoit, this shadowy stranger—what was he doing?"

"I could hardly see. It was very dark."

"Then you can't be sure it was Benoit," I said. "But the other person was Oliver?"

"Well," Furlap said, hesitating, "I'm pretty sure it was Oliver. They stayed in the shadows, definitely hiding and trying not to be seen. Of course, nothing gets by me."

"When was this?" I asked. "What time did you see them?"

"I don't know. It was the afternoon. Shadows were already creeping into the alley, and I was on my way to the Drip & Tipple. I just happened to pass by at the right moment."

"The right moment, my hiney," Henny muttered. "This is all a load of bunk. I can't trust anything you say about Benoit."

Furlap shrugged. "You're the one who wanted to ask questions. It's not my fault you don't like the answers. All I can tell you is I saw two men in that alley not long before Oliver was found dead. Now, if you'll excuse me, I have a fencing frog that needs consistent moisture conditioning."

We shuffled out of Peter Furlap's shop.

"Can't trust him," Henny grumbled. "Besides, Benoit would never wear an ugly trench coat. He's got too much style."

"I agree," Esme said. "I wouldn't put it past Peter to make up a story about Benoit."

"We can't take the chance that he's lying," I said. "If Benoit met Oliver in that alley the same day, we need to look into it. What were they doing meeting in the shadows?"

"We could go ask Benoit directly," Esme suggested.

"I think we need to get our bearings first," I said. "Let's retrace our steps and take a fresh look at the alleyway. Maybe we'll spot something we missed."

* * *

We stood at the mouth of the darkened alley, staring into the shadows. The spot where Oliver was found had been cleared, and only the trash dumpster remained. Despite the relative cleanliness of the alley, it still felt dirty. Icky. The memory of Oliver remained. I was sure Henny and Esme felt the same as they remained frozen beside me.

Esme dry-wrung her hands. "I'm not sure it's a good idea for us to be seen here. Remember what Theo said?"

At mention of Theo, a low growl emanated from Henny's throat. "Nonsense. Let's poke around." Despite the confidence in her voice, she remained at the entrance to the alleyway.

It was like facing Ms. Ruthie when she was on the warpath. I remembered it would all be over soon, so I mustered my courage and took one tentative step, then another, and another until I was standing next to the dumpster. I turned back toward the twins.

They exchanged glances. I suspected there was silent twin talk between them, because they gulped down their fear and followed me into the shadows.

"What are we looking for?" Esme asked, peering around as though the specter of Oliver might jump out at any moment.

"Anything, really," I said. "A clue, a parchment, a note, a confession..." I could hear the defeat in my voice as I said the words. What could we expect to find after the authorities had already combed through the alley? What could possibly be left?

Henny kicked the wheel of the rusty dumpster. "I'm sure Potts gave it a once-over, decided we were guilty, and is already writing up his report as we speak."

The area had certainly been given more than a once-over. The alley was clean—the only thing remaining was the dumpster. It even looked like the cobbles had been swept, and the brick walls of the adjoining buildings cleaned of any potential evidence. Even Astrid's back door had the sheen of freshly washed paint.

We looked around for a few minutes, bending low to check the ground that was cast in shadow.

"I can't see worth a darn," Henny said. "These old eyes are letting me down." She straightened and stretched with dramatic flair. "My aching back, too. Why can't I look for something up high instead?"

With these words, I joined Henny in looking not at the ground, but at eye level. From my vantage point next to the dumpster, the corner of two buildings came into focus beyond the mouth of the alley.

"What are those two buildings?" I pointed down the long, narrow span.

"Eh." Henny squinted toward the daylight. "That's Big Harv's place and a bit of Town Hall."

But it wasn't just the buildings I could see—there were windows. Windows that looked onto the alleyway.

"Do you think anyone could have seen from those windows?" I asked.

"We should ask Big Harv," Esme said. "He's usually got a lookout on everything."

"You mean he snoops," Henny said. "Unless he's locked himself in a hope chest or an antique toilet again."

"What about Town Hall? There had to be people working that day, and that window has a great vantage point. They would have seen anyone loitering at the mouth of the alley. We should go ask some questions."

"I don't think Mayor Theo would like that very much," Esme said. "She'd put a stop to it right quick."

"And she wouldn't like us peddling our wares there either," Henny said, "so we can't use that as a cover."

The familiar clank of a baton scraped against the bricks.

Constable Potts rounded the corner. "A cover for what?"

Henny let out an exasperated sigh. "Why are you always lurking about?"

Constable Potts' eyes narrowed. "It's my job to lurk. Now, what are you three doing back in this alley? Doesn't look good."

The appearance of the constable put a knot in my stomach. We didn't need him finding more reasons to suspect us of wrongdoing.

I held up the basket of salves. "We're just delivering to Ms. Starcaller. We always deliver to the back door, at her request."

The constable swung his baton leisurely in a wide circle at his waist. I could tell he was thinking this over.

To continue the ruse, I knocked on the back door of the Dreamnasium. A moment later, Astrid answered, swinging the door open with surprise in her eyes at finding the three of us—along with the constable—at her back door.

Before she could ask, I held up the basket full of salves. "We're here to deliver a reverse potion for Maude's Hair Apparent samples."

As soon as the words were out of my mouth, I noticed there was nothing wrong with her hair.

"Maude's samples?" Astrid repeated. "I never use anything made by that woman. I always order from the Meriweathers."

"We were just checking to make sure," I said, casting saddened eyes at the constable, whose free hand twitched toward his own scalp. "Many have suffered." His eyes darted away from mine. "Perhaps you would like one, Constable Potts? Just in case." I gave him a smile and proffered him a tiny container, which he took with a grunt of acknowledgment. It quickly disappeared into a pocket.

"She got to you too, eh?" Henny said, hiking up her pants with a satisfied grin.

"Well, if that's all then we'll be off," Esme said sweetly. "Toodles."

Astrid shut her door, and we scurried from the alleyway, as far from Constable Potts as possible. Like the day we discovered the body, we stopped along the sidewalk out of earshot, somewhat breathless at our ease of escape.

"Smart thinking, Carmody," Henny said. "No surprise Constable Potts would fall for Maude's faulty freebies. Probably palmed a handful and stuffed them in his uniform pocket when no one was looking."

Standing on the sidewalk, I spotted a pair of badged workers with an unnatural amount of hair emerging from the steps of Town Hall. My eyes followed as they crossed the street, heading toward the Drip & Tipple.

A quick plan came together in my mind. "If Theo won't let us into Town Hall, I think I know where we can find a few of her staff to question."

Henny and Esme spotted the two people.

"Good," Henny said. "I could go for a drink. And I'm sure the other masses of Drip & Tipple patrons will be sporting a few extra-long hairdos just waiting for our handy-dandy salve to save the day." She rubbed her hands together. "And we'll be in for a tidy profit."

Ten

HENNY PUSHED THROUGH the door of the Drip & Tipple, a wide smile on her face, no doubt dreaming of her whiskey and profits. But as soon as we stepped inside, the twangy, discordant notes of a poorly tuned musical instrument met our ears. Her smile faded. "Gads," she exclaimed. "Forgot it was open mic tonight. Fitzgibbon and his lyre are already tainting the stage. Find me a swizzle stick, Esme, so I can gouge out my eardrums."

"He's not that bad," Esme said with a titter. "He just needs to have it properly tuned."

"He's been plucking those strings since the last millennium. Surely, one's gotta give eventually."

Roanna waved at us from behind the counter. "The usuals?"

We met her at the bar and waited for our drinks. I couldn't deny the bubbling warmth inside me—not just from the thought of enjoying another chai, though that drink was magical. Part of it was something else: having the "usual" alongside Henny and Esme felt like being part of a family. It reminded me of my urgency to clear their names. My jaw set. I wouldn't go back to the orphanage.

Roanna clasped two steamy mugs and two-fingers of whiskey in her hands and placed them in front of us. "Anything new, ladies?"

Henny dug her hand into the basket full of potions at let them fall back like dribbles of water. "Here to offer your patrons some relief from a completely unsurprising Maude blunder."

"And to ask a few Town Hall employees some important questions," Esme added.

I grumbled internally. Roanna was still on my suspect list, no matter what Henny and Esme thought. The less she knew, the better.

"Pistol and Jean came in a minute ago." Roanna nodded toward a dark corner of the bar where a deep-seated booth was crammed against the wall.

The two people I'd seen crossing the street were snugged tightly into the booth, deep in conversation. The woman, who must be Jean, kept grabbing at the strands of flaxen hair falling over her shoulders. Pistol, nodding at whatever Jean was saying, pawed at his own hair, although it was jet black and tied back with a thick rubber band.

Henny took a slow sip of her whiskey and nodded. "That's them."

"What exactly are you questioning them on?" Roanna asked.

I piped up before Henny could spill any more beans. "Just a few things about the Town Hall building."

"G-good evening, ladies," came a weak voice from behind us.

It was Jasper, tall and skinny and meek, and though

he greeted us all, his eyes barely left Esme.

"Oh, hello Jasper." Esme's voice was breathy. "How nice to see you."

"I-I wanted to make sure you're feeling all right after the, ah, picnic."

Bless him, I thought. He only fumbled a few of the words getting them out.

Her eyelashes fluttered, and she ran her hand along the long braid draped over her shoulder. "I'm just fine, thanks to you, that is. Not sure how that fall would've ended if you hadn't been there to catch me."

"Yes," Henny drawled, swirling her whiskey. "Big, strong hero saved our little Esme from certain death." She clapped him on the shoulder, and he flinched from the force.

"N-not sure I'd call myself a hero." Jasper pushed on the bridge of his glasses. His eyes flitted to the floor as he twirled the brim of his hat nervously between his fingers.

He fumbled in his pocket and pulled out a crumpled piece of paper. "I've, ah, written a poem, Miss Esme. I h-hope you'll stay for open mic. Mr. Fitzgibbon should be done soon."

"God willing," Henny muttered.

Jasper frowned at the middle-aged man strumming his lyre enthusiastically on stage, no sign of stopping.

Esme shuffled her feet. "That sounds lovely. I can't wait to hear it."

Henny opened her mouth, but Roanna placed a hand on her forearm and shook her head.

"How about another drink, Jasper?" Roanna interjected. "Decaf tea with skim milk, was it?"

"Yes, th-thank you. It'll calm my nerves for the

stage." He let out a pained chortle, then choked back a gurgle as it caught in his throat.

He was braver than I'd ever be. I couldn't imagine sitting up on that stage with all those eyes on me. *He must be terrified.*

Jasper took his tea, nodded at us, and made his way toward the stage to wait out Fitzgibbon. A particularly sharp note pinged, ending the song, but Fitzgibbon moved straight into the next number.

"Writes his own stuff," Roanna said flatly. "Every. Open. Mic."

I grabbed the basket of salves, and we stepped away from the bar and convened near a post separating the two distinct sides of the Drip & Tipple.

"These Town Hall folk might run back to Theo and report our interrogation," Henny said.

"If you keep your cool," I said, "it might not be construed as an interrogation."

Henny gave me a look that said she didn't know what I meant by *her* keeping cool.

"We'll be nice and sweet and shouldn't raise any suspicions." Esme nodded as though it were that simple.

Our game plan was in place, but a final thwang from the lyre, followed by a smattering of half-hearted applause, announced the long-awaited end of Fitzgibbon's set.

"I think Jasper's taking the stage," Esme said, unable to hide the excitement in her voice.

"I guess that means I'll be interrogating alone," Henny muttered, rolling her eyes. "She'll be wrapped up in whatever nonsense Jasper's written."

The lanky man stepped onto the stage, clutching the

crumpled piece of paper in both trembling hands.

I grinned at Esme's enthusiasm. "I think it's sweet."

Henny rolled her eyes again and turned to head toward the booth, but she suddenly stopped and held a hand up in front of me.

"No minors allowed on that side. Stay here by this post. Should be close enough to overhear. Just act natural." She snatched the basket from my arms and stomped off.

I sighed and leaned against the post, keeping an eye on Pistol and Jean from my vantage point. Henny strolled up to their booth in a decidedly unnatural gait looking entirely suspicious.

"Evening, you two," Henny greeted them, her voice overly cheerful. They tensed visibly.

"What do you want, Henrietta Meriweather?" Jean asked through a frown.

"Can't I come by to say hello?"

Jean smirked. "Since when have you ever come by to say hello?"

Henny bristled. "There's a first time for everything, isn't there?"

I groaned internally. Expecting Henny to be as sweet as honey was like expecting a badger to curl up in your lap for a cozy nap.

Henny said her next few words through gritted teeth. "I see you've both got impressive manes of flowing locks today. You wouldn't happen to have slathered on a free sample from Elix Mix recently?"

Pistol and Jean exchanged more frowns.

"And what if we did?" Pistol asked.

Henny jostled the basket, making the jars clink

together. "Just so happens I have a solution to that pesky problem."

"And what do you want for them?" Jean asked warily.

Henny rocked back on her heels with a sly smile. "Oh, just a little information about Town Hall."

"Theo doesn't like us talking about our work," Pistol said.

Henny jangled the basket again and raised her eyebrows.

"What do you want to know?" Jean asked.

I repositioned myself by the post, leaning as far over as I dared to catch the conversation. I tried to project my voice and whisper-shouted, "Ask if there's a video." Henny didn't react.

In the meantime, Jasper had gathered his nerves and was clearing his throat at the microphone. I was torn between his poem and supervising Henny's rocky interrogation.

"A little birdie told me Pistol's a bit of a voyeur," Henny said. "Likes to stare out the window at people."

I cringed. Insulting our witnesses wasn't going to help.

"Who told you that?" Pistol snapped.

"Don't worry about it," Henny shot back. "I want to know if you saw anything the afternoon Oliver was murdered. That alley's right in view from your window."

Jasper's voice warbled over the microphone, unsteady but sincere, *"Your eyes are two shimmering puddles of brown water. Your braid the thick gray hair of an aging Rapunzel. Your skin the marbled..."*

Yeesh. I turned back just in time to catch the end of

Pistol's reply.

"—wearing a trench coat. I mean, it's May. Who wears a trench coat in May?"

Trench coat? What had I missed?

"We told all this to Constable Potts already." Jean said. "Why do *you* care?"

Henny plucked two vials of salve from the basket and clutched them in her closed palm. "I've got two reasons for you not to care why I care." She slapped the salves on the table, drawing curious glances from nearby patrons.

I groaned.

"Did you see anything else? Any video? CCTV that might've caught this person on tape?"

Yes! Whether Henny had heard me or not, she was on the right track. A video would not only show this trench-coated person but also clear Roanna and Astrid if it showed her entering the Dreamnasium. Maybe even capture the actual murder.

I leaned further in, but a particularly emotive surge of sound from the stage overwhelmed their faint voices.

"*...a summertime stroll through a meadow with no ticks or allllergies...*"

Henny leaned on the table, looming over Pistol and Jean. "Did either of you see Benoit or Peter Furlap in that alley?"

"There's no way to make out faces from that far away," Jean grumbled. "And besides, we're half-asleep most of the time. Theo's got us working overtime. We were lucky to clock out at a normal time today."

"Why is that?"

"She wants to make up for Oliver's lost income. He was one of the biggest revenue sources for the city."

"No kidding," Henny said flatly.

"...slow dancing without stepping on your toes. Staring down the length of your slightly crooked nose..."

Jean nodded. "Theo may not be panicking yet, but she'll be in a big budget crunch without Oliver's consistent over-achieving to balance the scales."

Theo needed Oliver? This new information changed my perspective on the mayor and her motive.

My train of thought was broken by the most abominable screeching coming from the side of the stage. My attention was pulled in time to see Erebus, the fluffy black pegacat, bound onto the stage. Jasper let out a startled wail as Erebus darted across his feet toward the other side.

Then I spotted him. Or *it*.

Nuts dashed only a few feet ahead of the pegacat but crashed into an unsupervised cup of tea left on the edge of the stage, sending shards of porcelain and hot liquid scattering across the floor. Erebus was not deterred.

Roanna's deep bellow filled the room, "Get him!" She snatched a broom leaning against a wall and leaped over the counter in one athletic hop.

Nuts, spotting the attack, tried to turn an about-face, his tiny claws scraping for purchase on the wood of the stage.

Roanna swung the broom, but not before Nuts dashed out of the way in a flurry of fur.

Just then, a swath of light streamed across the floor as an unsuspecting patron opened the door to the pub.

The squirrel made his move. He zipped through human and table legs like a prized agility dog and escaped, unscathed, to the street.

Henny appeared beside me. "What's all the racket?"

"Nuts, but he got away." I waved a hand toward the door.

A low growl started in Henny's throat. "Not just Nuts."

I followed her glare. Hidden behind the edge of the stage, a mop of unruly brown curls poked from the shadows. Boyd.

Esme scurried from her spot closer to the stage, cheeks dewy and eyelashes fluttering. "Wasn't it wonderful? Jasper wrote it himself—" Her words cut off at the sight of Henny's glowering face. "Nuts didn't mean any harm, I'm sure."

"Not Nuts." Henny pointed toward the shadows. "Boyd's hiding over there like a sewer rat. Furlap must have set him up to spy on us."

"That's a bit of a leap. The poor boy's just…" but Esme's words trailed off.

"Just what? Grabbing a pint? Sitting down for a three-course meal? The lad hasn't got two coins to rub together. And don't forget he was here with Nuts. That's a sure sign he's up to no good."

Henny's words made me feel for the boy. I didn't have two coins to rub together either. "Maybe he's just looking for some fun. I can't imagine he gets much of that around Mr. Furlap. Why don't you tell us what you learned, Henny? I only overheard a little. Something about a trench coat?"

Henny nodded at this. "Pistol spotted two men meeting in the alleyway not long before the murder. One in a long trench coat, the other hidden from view. Too far to see faces, anyway."

"How does he know either of them were men?" I

asked.

"He...uh." Henny scratched her head. "I didn't ask that."

I filed away that mental note. "That confirms Peter's story, at least. Go on."

"Says the guy in the trench coat did a good job of hiding his face. Pistol got a call and missed the rest of whatever went on. When he got back, the men were gone."

"Gosh," Esme said. "That sounds suspicious."

"Any chance of a video?" I asked.

Henny shook her head. "That's a negative. Apparently, Theo canceled the security service to save money. At least, that's the rumor. Probably stuff the savings into her own pockets."

"Then we'll have to try Big Harv's again," I said. "Maybe he has a security system."

"Oh, he does," Esme said. "Wee Harv, remember?"

I had to admit that boulder of a man would dispossess anyone of thoughts of theft. But heavyweight or not, he wouldn't take the place of capturing this clandestine alleyway meeting on video. "We have to feel out this lead. We have to at least ask."

Henny appeared doubtful. "There's a slim-to-nil chance Big Harv would splurge on a security system. The man's a card-carrying tightwad."

I looked to Esme for support.

Esme sighed. "Carmody's right. We should at least check."

Henny crossed her arms. "Fine, but if Big Harv gets feisty, I'm stuffing him back into that wardrobe and feeding the key to one of Benoit's were-rabbits."

Eleven

I AWOKE THE following morning with the nightmare still pounding in my head. I'd been chased by a broom down a dark alley where Ms. Ruthie waited for me, a scolding finger wagging from above.

Rolling out of bed, I sat at the edge, letting the nightmare drift away as dreams do. The sinking feeling remained, leaving me ill and disoriented. I palmed the sleep from my eyes and shook off the remnants of the memory.

My tower room was a comfort. It was bright, airy, a bit drafty—but not a darkened alley, and certainly devoid of Ms. Ruthie.

I dressed quickly, still mostly asleep, pulling on my oversized trousers and threw on the shirt I'd worn yesterday, only to spot a chai stain smack in the center.

Somewhere in this room was my other good shirt. My arrival had felt like such a whirlwind, and I couldn't remember where I'd stored anything in this unfamiliar space, so I poked through the dresser drawers searching for where I'd stashed it.

I jerked open the bottom drawer, fully expecting my

neatly folded shirt, but it wasn't there. Instead, a thick tome, stuck deep into the recesses, slid forward and hit the edge, letting off a plume of dust. It must have been dislodged from the force of my tug.

I picked it up and blew away the layer of grime, then ran my fingers along the weathered, midnight-blue leather cover. Every bump and groove of the border of embossed scrolls spoke to its age. *How long have you been hiding in there?*

Most curiously, at the center of the front cover was a shallow depression. Just a dip, a small divot, the patina worn smooth from years of handling.

I rushed to my bed, where the light from the window was better. The hinges squeaked as I plopped onto the mattress.

Immediately, I moved to open the book, curious as to its contents, but the cover wouldn't budge. I turned the book around in my hand, looking for a clasp or a lock, something that would be securing it closed, but there was nothing there. Just two thick covers and the rough, deckle edge of the pages.

Then I spotted the initials. At a certain angle of the light, their impression was revealed, tooled into the leather of the back cover.

"M.M.," I murmured.

Could this belong to the mysterious third Meri-weather sister? The one I wasn't supposed to ask about, speak about, or even think about?

The stomp of heavy footfalls pounded on the stair-well leading up to my tower. Henny.

I had three seconds to find a hiding spot for the secret book, finally slipping it under a discarded print-out for

Module 1.2.

I popped up, ready to greet Henny, but my eyes fell on Maude's freebie perched boldly on the nightstand for all to see. My hand darted out, and I tucked the salve into my trouser pocket just as the door opened.

"Good morning, Car—" Henny stopped. "You all right?"

"What? Me? Yes. I'm fine. Fine."

She frowned and at the same time, her twitchy eye twitched.

"Just tired," I said to reassure her.

"Mm-hmm," she muttered. Her eyes scanned the room. Finally, she said, "Breakfast is ready. See you downstairs."

She turned to go, and I let out a hushed sigh of relief. Then she turned back.

I stiffened, waiting for her inevitable pronouncement of my dishonesty, disobedience, and downright disloyalty to the honorable Meriweather name.

Henny pointed an accusing finger straight at me.

A lump rose in my throat.

"You've got a stain," she said. "Right there on your shirt."

Two minutes later, greatly relieved and with my soiled shirt replaced, I arrived downstairs.

"Good heavens, my dear, you look like you've been hit by a train."

"Just about," I said. "Bad dream about that alley-way."

Esme tsked. "We should have never gotten you into that terrible mess. With all this death going around, we should be focusing on your studies instead. We received an email from the Association this morning telling us to expect a visit to assess your progress."

My stomach dropped. "My progress?"

Henny scoffed. "We've already got you perfecting hair reduction salves—that's basically third-level tingling. Can't wait to see the assessor's face when they hear about that."

"Now, I don't want to downplay your achievement, dear," Esme said. "But we should be much further along in your formal studies by now. We've barely touched Module 2.4 and should be on Module 3.3 by now."

"There's plenty of time for studying," Henny said. "I'm eager to check on Big Harv, see if he's got any cameras trained on the alleyway."

"Don't you think Constable Potts would have confiscated any video if it existed?" I asked.

"Constable Potts has his head so far up Theo's re-election campaign, I doubt he knows which way is up. No, Carmody zipped through that salve like butter, no lesson needed. Like I said, they'll be thoroughly impressed with her progress. Blown away, in fact."

Esme glanced at the pile of printed-out training modules next to her on the table. She sighed, then patted the stack of papers. "I guess these could wait until later."

* * *

We gave the outside of Big Harv's warehouse a thorough look-over. To our surprise, a security camera was mounted on the top corner, facing in the general direction of the alleyway where Oliver was murdered.

"Unbelievable," Henny said with a tinge of wonder.

"Big Harv actually has some scruples."

"This could bode very well," Esme said. "Let's remember to be polite when we ask to see the tape." She glanced at Henny. "And ask nicely."

"I'm always polite," Henny said. "Besides, Big Harv's got the hots for me. All I'll have to do is ask, and he'll produce."

I wasn't sure that was the case, but I appreciated Henny's confidence.

We entered the warehouse just as before. The same layer of grime coated every piece of furniture crammed into the tight space. We followed the carved-out path through dressers, chairs, and armoires toward the small transaction window set into the back wall.

A bright red caution sign had been taped to the front of the hungry armoire—the one that had tried to eat Big Harv the last time we were here. It must have gotten even more out of control.

"I wonder if there's a wood stain or a wax finish that might calm that armoire down?"

Esme tittered. "That's a wonderful idea, my dear. I never thought of that."

"We could probably get a pretty penny off Big Harv for it," Henny said. "We'll keep that in our back pocket for later."

At the mention of pockets, my hand twitched to my side, feeling the distinct outline of Maude's Hair Apparent, still hiding there from this morning.

Big Harv appeared through a door next to the transaction window and startled when he spotted us standing next to the caution-taped armoire.

"Back away from that," he said. "I won't be held

liable for your snooping around."

"Calm down," Henny said. "We're just here to ask about your cameras."

"My what?"

"The security cameras mounted on the building outside," I said. "We noticed you had one trained on the alleyway."

Big Harv scratched at his chin with one grimy finger. "Eh, forgot about that."

"Well?" Henny pressed. "Can we see the tape? You could have caught Oliver's murderer on it."

His eyes bulged, then quickly shifted. "Tape's not working."

Henny slapped a hand to her thigh. "I knew it. I knew you wouldn't have your act together."

"I used to have a working camera," he said defensively. "Thing broke about a year ago. Didn't bother getting it fixed. It deters all the same." His eyes narrowed. "Don't you go telling anyone that. If they find out, I'll know it was you who squealed."

"Well, that's just great," Henny said. "Big help you are."

Esme let out a great sigh. "It was worth a shot. At least we got some information from Pistol and Jean about the man in the trench coat."

Big Harv leaned in a little closer. "Trench coat?"

"That's right," I said. "We were hoping to find video of who was meeting a man in a trench coat in that alleyway earlier in the day. Even better if the video could catch Oliver's killer."

"I guess this means we can't confirm Roanna visited Astrid either," Esme said, disheartened.

A hulking figure leaned into view, hidden behind the armoire. It was Wee Harv.

"Roanna?" he asked slowly. "I saw Roanna."

Henny perked up. "You did? When did you see her? Where?"

"Dad sent me on an errand to—"

"Don't you go talking," Big Harv cut in.

Henny waved him off. "Go ahead, Wee."

The big man shifted his eyes from his father to Henny as if asking for permission to continue. "She went into the Dreamnasium."

I turned to Henny and Esme. "If Wee Harv saw Roanna go into the Dreamnasium, that bodes well for their alibis."

I glanced at Wee Harv. "When did you see Roanna?"

He furrowed his brow and took a moment to respond. "About three."

I spun back to the twins. "That's right before the murder."

Esme clapped her tiny hands together. "This bodes *very* well for Roanna."

I turned back to Wee Harv. "Did you see Roanna leaving?"

He shook his massive head. "No. Off on my errand by then."

"All right." Big Harv stepped between us and Wee. "That's enough questions. Any more and I'll have to charge you Wee's hourly rate."

He shooed us out, waggling his hands until we retreated down the path of furniture and left.

Esme brushed a bit of dust off her clothes. "He seemed awfully pushy."

"Big Harv is always pushy," Henny said. "Doesn't want anyone in his shop unless he's got a potential sale. At least we got info on Roanna."

I was relieved to find out that Roanna was telling us the truth, but as promising as this new information was, it was still open-ended. The question now was, could Roanna and Astrid have been working together?

* * *

The three of us stopped dead on the sidewalk. Far ahead, a figure peered into the window of the Meriweathers' potion shop. From the stiff suit and skinny, pressed tie, I knew he must be from the American Association of Potion Makers. My stomach lurched. This man's opinion could send me back to the orphanage. Send me back to Ms. Ruthie.

"Is that him?" Esme wailed. "So soon? We only got notice today." She shuffled in her tote for the module pages and pulled them out in a messy handful. "Henny, let me handle this for once."

As we approached, the man adjusted his glasses and peered down at us. His movements reminded me of Oliver: slinky and sly.

"Good morning," Esme said. "Can we help you?" Her hopeful tone that this man could be anyone other than the Association's representative was quickly brushed off a cliff.

He flicked two deft fingers into the breast pocket of his jacket and produced a slick business card.

We huddled together over the card.

"Gerald Honeywell, Senior Compliance Officer,

A.A.P.M. Youth Internship Program." Henny read each word with pointed suspicion.

"And I assume you two are the Meriweather Potion Masters?" He inched his glasses down his nose with a bony finger. "And this must be…" He checked the notes on his clipboard. "Carmody Greene."

I gulped. The sheer level of glare I felt with his eyes upon me was enough to send me running. "Yes, sir," I managed to sputter.

"Very well, let us proceed. I'm sure you're expecting me, although I rather expected you to be present to greet me when I arrived. An empty potion shop does not bode well for Ms. Greene's progress in actual potion making."

Esme laughed nervously and pawed at the module papers in her bag. "Certainly sir, er, Mr. Honeywell. We've got the curriculum right here, ready to go."

Henny stepped right up to the officer. "I think you'll be pleasantly surprised, Honeydew—"

The man's mouth tightened. "Honeywell."

"Right, right" Henny said. "You'll be impressed to hear that young Carmody has already had her first breakthrough in the cauldron."

A skeptical eyebrow rose an inch or two. "Is that so?" Eyes on me again.

Esme fumbled for her keys and we shuffled into the shop. Mr. Honeywell followed, his gait confident, each step as judgmental as the next.

As Henny and Esme scuttled around the shop, straightening bottle displays and clearing toppling piles of loose papers into more structurally sound piles of random papers, Mr. Honeywell's eyes flowed from one grimy spot near the door in a sharp arc at every imperfection I'd never noticed until that very moment. A dribble of spilled potion on the corner of a display case, a set of salves that had toppled over, that spot on the wall where an overexcited customer had pulled the stopper from her shaken vial of Enduring Energy Elixir and it had exploded, spraying onto every surface.

Mr. Honeywell's indecipherable mumbled was quite easy to decipher.

"Why don't we make our way to the workroom?" Esme's easy, kind voice belied the nervousness I knew bubbled beneath the surface.

At mention of the workroom, Henny and I both grimaced. If Mr. Honeywell thought the public-facing shop portion was in disarray, he was about to be sorely surprised at the private work space.

The memory of my first day in the shop sprung back into my mind. Mr. Honeywell's intense scrutiny of the establishment mirrored Oliver's fastidious perusal of every nook and cranny. And like Oliver, Compliance Officer Gerald Honeywell had the ability to take this all away from me.

Esme drew back the curtain, and the ragged gurgle from the man's throat was sign enough that things were going south.

"Now, Mr. Compliance Officer, sir," Esme said as she rushed to straighten the nearest toppling pile of empty potion bottles, "it's not normally like this, but you'll see we've got all the proper equipment and safety measures in place."

Mr. Honeywell cleared his throat. "That remains to be seen. However, what I'm most interested in is how far Ms. Greene's studies have progressed. I will begin with a series of questions. Are you ready, Ms. Greene?"

I gulped hard as he latched his steely eyes onto me. "Yes, sir."

"What two ingredients constitute the most common blend for a base potion?"

The gears in my mind spun rapidly, recalling each instance I'd been in the workroom, each swirl of the big spoon, each gentle encouragement from Esme and each push from Henny. But no matter how hard I tried to remember, I couldn't grasp a memory of any conversation regarding potion bases. Had we covered that module? How could that have been overlooked? I began to regret falling in line with Henny's eagerness to solve Oliver's murder at the expense of my training.

Honeywell tapped the corner of his clipboard, waiting for my response. "Ms. Greene? The two ingredients, if you please."

From the corner of my eye, Henny hopped from foot to foot, grinding her teeth and clenching her fists in time. She was frustrated with me. My heart sank. I was letting them down.

Dig Carmody. You know this. You've heard this somewhere. But where? I blinked back the emergence of tears, my own frustration taking hold.

"You're doing just fine, dear." Esme beamed me a reassuring smile.

Potion base. Potion base. I dug through my memories.

Behind Mr. Honeywell, Henny mimed stirring something, then pinched at her stomach. Whatever she was trying to tell me, it wasn't working.

"This is quite a basic question." He shook his head

sadly. "I'm afraid we'll have to—"

"Wait, please," I begged. "Just another moment."

He raised an eyebrow at my request, but settled back into waiting for my answer.

Memories, memories. Arriving, Oliver, the Drip & Tipple, Nuts, the gala, Elix Mix, and… *yes!*—Henny racing through common blends on the walk to Big Harv's.

"The two ingredients are ground marigold seeds and cotton lint." I finalized my answer with a confident nod of my head and a grin from ear to ear.

Mr. Honeywell's other eyebrow rose. "That is correct."

Esme clapped her hands together in soft applause.

Henny gave Esme's shoulder a hearty shake. "Knew she had it in her the whole time."

"Next question." Honeywell stared at me down his long nose. "What are the main ingredients in a Love Potion?"

Love Potion? But Esme said—

My shoulders stiffened. "There is no known recipe or a Love Potion. In addition, there are strict Association guidelines restricting potions of that sort."

He nodded and made a quick notation on his clipboard.

Behind Honeywell, Esme beamed and clapped her delicate hands together. "Oh, well done, Carmody."

"Very well," Honeywell said. "I would now like to test the progress of Ms. Greene's tingling. According to the curriculum, a basic potion should be no problem at this stage."

My confidence was growing after answering Mr. Honeywell's questions, but now came the real test. I'd only successfully mixed one potion—the hair reduction potion. Could I tingle again? I clenched my hands and wiggled my fingers to warm them up.

The man turned to Esme. "Ms. Meriweather, please retrieve the following ingredients from your stores: dried lacewing, salamander slime, cardamom, and sixteen ounces of distilled water."

Esme rushed off and soon returned with an armful of ingredients. "We're out of the salamander slime, so I pulled toad bile instead. That should substitute for what I think you're going for."

Mr. Honeywell nodded. "That will suffice." He waved for Esme to set the ingredients on the table next to the fire pit. "Now, Ms. Greene, please concoct a basic potion to treat upset stomachs using the ingredients provided. This should have been covered in Module 2.2: *Rudimentary Tinctures and Tonics.*"

I perked up at this request. Henny and Esme had walked me through their Tummy Trouble potion in one of my first lessons. Then my heart sank. What if I couldn't tingle at all? Last time felt like a fluke. Even Henny and Esme had been surprised the salve turned out so well. But there was only one way to find out.

First, I grabbed the appropriate-sized stainless-steel cauldron and set the fire. While that heated up, I found a mortar and pestle and the largest cherry wood spoon off the wall of tools.

The lacewing and cardamom needed to be ground to a smooth paste. As I mashed, Mr. Honeywell jotted notes in his report, taking notice of my technique, no doubt.

I poured the paste into the cauldron along with a hefty goop of toad bile, then slowly added the distilled water. The mixture began to bubble, big blobs of green goo roiling to the top then burst in a magnificent splatter, all contained within the confines of the perfectly sized cauldron I'd selected. I spared a glance at Henny and Esme, who nodded back at me. So far so good.

The spoon felt heavy in my hands, but I leaned over the mixture and stirred three times, careful to ensure I was moving clockwise. I wondered what counter-clockwise would produce, but now was not the time for wandering thoughts. By the third stir, the potion had thickened, just as it had in my first lesson.

I set the spoon aside and pulled up my sleeves, rubbed my hands together, then held out my arms over the cauldron and closed my eyes.

The meadow spread before me in full bloom. In the dusky light, the flits of insects stood out against the skies and backdrop of dappled trees surrounding the glade. Birds chirped. Or was it crickets?

Focus.

Crickets chirped, unseen, from the tall grasses. My hands stretched before me, tickling the tops of the grasses and wild flowers. I let all sensation fade until only the sharp note of a single cricket remained. A warmth rose, clear and strong in the tips of my fingers, then grew to a white-hot heat. I urged the tingle from my fingers, urged it to release, not just to ease the burn, but to prove I could do it. I was a potion maker, and Mr. Honeywell was going to know it.

Energy coursed through my fingers, flowing toward the tip, collecting, burning, scorching my skin. I wanted to scream from the pain.

A flare of white light behind my eyelids shook me

from my trance. I stumbled back from the cauldron, but Esme's gentle hands caught me before I could fall. I eased into her shoulder to catch my breath while the burning faded from my hands.

Honeywell appeared bewildered, stunned, his mouth hanging slightly agape and eyes wide as they stared at me. He caught himself and quickly regained his stodgy composure. He dipped a vial into the potion and held it up a few inches from his face. The acid-green mixture swirled as he shook it and a fizz of bubbles rose to the top, threatening to overspill the tiny glass. "Extraordinary." His voice was barely a whisper. "So clear."

"Of course it's clear." Henny muscled her way to Honeywell's side and snatched the vial from his hands, giving it a close inspection herself. "She's under the expert tutelage of two Level Ten Potion Masters. What'd you expect?"

"I… I suppose I expected the skill of an intern. As much as it surprises me to say it, this potion is near perfection."

Esme rubbed my arms encouragingly. "Did you hear that, Carmody? *Near perfection.*"

Still too dazed to appreciate what had just happened, I only nodded.

Mr. Honeywell completed his forms with a bewildered look on his face. When he handed the copy to Henny, he shook his head as if he didn't believe what he'd just witnessed.

Henny grinned smugly back at him. "You tell the Association that the Meriweather twins have everything under control."

"I certainly will." He turned back to me. "You have

an exceptional gift, Ms. Greene. Keep up your studies and you're sure to excel. I expect to see great things from you in the future."

As the door shut behind him, I nearly melted into Esme's arms. *Exceptional gift. Great things.*

And I had absolutely no idea what I'd done.

Twelve

ONCE THE COMPLIANCE officer had left, Henny couldn't stop gloating about how we'll I'd performed. "I bet the entire Association will know about our intern by the end of the day."

"You were very impressive, Carmody," Esme said. "We're so proud of you."

"And how she cut down Honeycomb's trick question." Henny mimed a karate chop.

"Honeywell," I corrected.

"You know who needs to hear about this?" Henny rubbed her hands together. "Maude."

Esme cleared her throat. "Perhaps we should capitalize on this momentum and dive into Carmody's next module."

"Nonsense. She needs to recover after that exertion." Henny picked up the basket of the remaining hair reduction salves. "Let's pay Maude a visit. I'm sure there are some residual suckers begging her for a solution to their hair trouble."

A few nauseating minutes later, Henny squealed the

tuk-tuk tires into a spot outside of Elix Mix. She hopped from the driver's seat and headed for the shop door with jaunty steps. Esme and I followed in her gleeful wake.

Maude's two simpering staff leaned against the back counter, their low energy far from the bustling business I'd observed a few short days ago.

"What nice big hats you have, ladies." Henny plopped the basket of salves onto the counter. "You suddenly appear to have an abundance of hair. Might I interest you in—"

Maude appeared from around a corner. She took in the scene before glowering at her lethargic employees. She pointed at Henny's basket. "What on Earth is this?"

"Salves, Maude. Or should I say, your *salv*ation." Henny chuckled at her own joke.

"I don't need saving, thank you very much."

Henny pointed at the oversized hats atop her employees' heads.

Maude ground her teeth. "I'm working on a solution right now."

Henny patted the side of the basket. "Carmody's already created a perfect solution. In fact, we've just had a visit from the Association. Carmody's flying through her training. Said she had an *exceptional gift*."

"I wouldn't say she's flying through…" Esme's words trailed off.

"Is that so?" Maude eyed me up and down. "I suppose next you'll be alchemizing gold or crafting a truth serum? Perhaps discovering the elixir of life itself?"

"No need to patronize," Esme said. "We're very proud of what she's accomplished."

Henny waggled a hand at the two women behind the

counter. "And your hirsute noodles over there don't appear to be doing much of anything."

Maude's jaw hardened, then she waved for the two employees to go, and they quickly skittered out of sight.

"All right, Meriweathers. What do you really want? I'm very busy."

"If it's your miracle solution you're busy with," Henny said, "don't waste your time. You can just buy ours."

"The recipe?"

Henny threw her head back. "Ha! Even if you knew the recipe, you couldn't possibly tingle this level of potency."

Maude folded her arms and leaned back against a display case. "Not interested."

"No? And what happens when the next Hair Apparent victim shows up and you don't have answers?"

"It was a slight miscalculation in the formula for—"

"Slight?" Henny guffawed. "You've turned the town into a prancing pony show. They'll want solutions, not excuses."

Maude's mouth worked into a knot. "I don't want your potion or your perfect intern or your… your…"

"Perhaps we should go." Esme laid a hand on Henny's arm. "Maude appears to be apoplectic."

"Fine, fine." Henny snatched the basket off the counter. "If any of your dupes come sniffing around, send them our way."

"Oh, just get out!"

Henny, quite pleased with herself, radiated glee as we left Elix Mix. "I think that went well, don't you?"

"You shouldn't rile her up, Henny. And I shouldn't

have let you bring us along."

"Don't be such a wet sock, Esme. I can't believe Maude thinks she's going to come up with some marvelous reversal potion. And she's clearly jealous of our intern." Henny slapped me on the back.

I jolted from the force. "Thank you."

"All right, let's go," Henny said. "As usual Maude was stubborn and entirely useless."

But something Maude had said had stuck in my mind, a tiny kernel of an idea. I certainly wasn't going to transform pewter into gold or stumble upon the elixir of eternal life, but…

"What about a truth serum?" I asked.

Henny and Esme blinked at me.

"You know, a truth serum so we can just ask and know who killed Oliver?"

"Truth serums don't exist dear," Esme said. "It's one of those pie-in-the-sky potions. Simply a legend or a myth like the Love Potion."

My shoulders sank. Of course something so obvious would have been considered by now. It was silly of me to even suggest. Just an hour ago I'd stood before the Association Compliance Officer and lectured *him* on mythical Love Potions. All we could do was reverse effects, like correcting Hair Apparent, or do the opposite, like the Leave Potion the Meriweathers made for— *Wait! The opposite?*

"What about the opposite of a truth serum?" I asked. "It does the reverse. It makes people lie. Like how Jody Halverson's Leave Potion was the opposite of a Love Potion."

Their mouths worked silently, digesting this

question.

I explained further. "If we could hear the opposite of the truth, that's nearly as good as the truth, right?"

Esme tapped her chin. "I suppose we could modify our children's low dose Fib Finder recipe."

"An *Untruth Serum*," Henny said. "I like this idea."

"We could use it on anyone," I said. "Find out what they really know. Or don't know, I guess."

Henny shimmied her way into the driver's seat of the tuk-tuk. "Let's hit the cauldron."

* * *

We rounded the corner and the Meriweather shop I'd come to call home came into view. My eyes instinctively went to the window of the tower high above. My window. Home. With the Association assessment behind me, my prospects looked good. I wiggled my fingers to make sure they were still working.

Henny screeched the tuk-tuk to a halt.

"What is it?" I asked.

She nodded toward the shop. "Furlap's rugrat is poking around again."

Sure enough, Boyd's scruffy head of hair peered through a window into the shop's interior, barely peeking above the sill.

"Oh dear," Esme said with a tsk. "He must be spying for Peter again."

"Stay here." Henny slithered from the tuk-tuk and stalked across the street with steps as quiet as a cat. I didn't think it possible for Henny to embody silence, yet here she was, stealthily tip-toeing to ambush an unsuspecting child.

She nabbed him by the scruff of his collar and gave him a shake.

"Oh dear," Esme said. "Perhaps we should intervene?"

But I was already ahead of Esme, making my way toward the two. Esme scuttled after me on her tiny feet.

As I approached, Boyd's big, desperate eyes latched onto me and he began to squirm in Henny's clutches.

"Hold on there, Henny," I said. "Let the kid go. He hasn't done anything wrong."

"Pokin' around for old Furlap, are you?" Henny tightened her grip on his collar. "Probably spying for Maude, too, eh?"

Boyd shook his head, moppy hair shaking wildly. "I-I weren't, I swear it, Miss Meriweather."

"Sure looks like it from here."

"For heaven's sake, Henny," Esme said, her voice out of breath from hustling across the street. "Let the poor child go."

I placed a hand on Henny's arm and she loosened her grip before releasing him with a disgusted "pah."

The boy adjusted his dirty, over-sized shirt to fix the collar. Henny's iron grip had probably given it a permanent wrinkle. "I weren't spying," he said to me, avoiding eye contact.

"I never said you were. So, what were you doing?"

"Well, I were…"

I crossed my arms, expecting an answer.

Boyd shuffled his feet. "Mr. Furlap sent me to spy on—"

"I knew it, you little toad!" Henny lunged, but he

skirted her attack.

"Not on you," he added quickly. "Mr. Furlap sent me to watch that animal fella."

"Benoit?" Esme blinked. "Why him?"

Boyd shrugged. "Said he wanted to know what the guy was up to."

Henny clenched her fists. "Course he did, that slimy snake. Wait until I get my hands on his hoity-toity—"

Esme shot her a silencing glare.

While Henny recovered from her fit, I wondered if Boyd may be just what we needed. "Boyd, have you ever spied on Benoit before?"

The boy shifted from foot to foot. "Sure, loads of times."

Henny choked back another snarl.

I rounded on Henny and Esme. "Benoit's Menagerie is near the Dreamnasium. Maybe he saw something that could clear Roanna."

That woke them up. Henny's face shifted to sweetness and pie, while Esme exclaimed a barely audible "oh."

"You wouldn't happen to be spying the day Oliver Oliphant was killed, were you?"

The toe of one worn shoe ground into the sidewalk. "Maybe."

"Well," Henny growled, all sticky sweetness quickly gone, "did you see anything?"

His eyes darted from me to Henny then Esme. "Maybe."

I leaned in closer, nearly a whisper in his ear. "Would you tell me? You won't get in trouble."

He swallowed hard, gulping down whatever shred of

fear remained. "I seen Mr. Oliphant, I did. He went into that dome place."

"Do you remember when, dear?" Esme asked.

Boyd glanced at me as if to check that it was okay to answer. I nodded.

"Suppose it were about three. Not too sure. Then I seen Miss Roanna go inside."

Esme's breath caught. "Astrid, Roanna *and* Oliver? They must have all been in the Dreamnasium right before Oliver was murdered."

Boyd shrugged. "Suppose so."

I spun on Henny and Esme. "Are you thinking what I'm thinking?"

"You suspect the two of them…" Esme said in a whisper.

"No way." Henny shook her head. "No chance."

"I know you don't think Roanna is capable," I said, "and I won't push that, but we could use the Untruth Serum on Astrid. Then we'll know for sure."

Henny nodded in agreement, then turned back to Boyd. "Did you see anything else, kid?"

He shook his head, curls flopping. "That's all I got. Fell asleep after that. Only woke up when Mr. Furlap found me an' boxed my ears. Didn't even see that animal guy all day, so I sat there for nothin'."

I winced. Memories of Ms. Ruthie's belt came flooding back.

"What did Constable Potts say when you told him this?" Esme asked. "Surely he'd want to know Oliver's whereabouts."

"Potts? He always says nothin' coming from me'd be worth beans, and he never asked, so I kept me mouth shut." He finalized this with a decisive nod. "I ain't told him nothin'."

I smiled down at Boyd. "Well, I think what you've told us is worth a *ton* of beans. Thanks for trusting us enough to share."

Boyd averted his eyes and stubbed at the ground with the tip of his worn shoe. "Gee, anythin' for you, Miss Carmody."

I gave Henny and Esme a satisfied grin. *Pure honey.*

* * *

With Boyd sent along his way, we began gathering the ingredients for the Untruth Serum only to find that we were missing a vital component.

"Salamander slime." Esme's shoulders wilted. "And this time, there's no substitution."

"How long 'til the order comes in?" Henny asked.

"It's on backorder. There just isn't any available."

I plopped onto a nearby stool. *So much for that idea.*

Henny threw her hands up. "There's got to be some way to get our hands on some slime."

"What about Maude?" I offered.

"Not likely, dear, especially after Henny's antics at Elix Mix earlier."

Henny glowered, but said nothing. Perhaps she'll hold her tongue once in a while now that her actions have come back to bite her.

"There is another option," I said. "It might be a long shot."

"I'll take anything you've got," Henny said.

"Benoit's menagerie. Maybe he has a salamander."

Two shakes later and we were headed down the street to Benoit's Exotic Pet Menagerie. I'd seen the shop before, as we sputtered by in the tuk-tuk and times we'd walked to the Drip & Tipple. Except for the green neon parrot sign flashing in the broad windows, I'd barely had an opportunity to glance inside to notice much about the shop.

Now, as we approached, I was able to see through the windows into the bustling little space beyond. Along with the neon parrot, Benoit's pegacat perched on the sill staring out at the passersby.

"Hello Erebus," I said through the glass. He blinked twice in response.

Esme craned her neck to get a better look inside. "I wonder if Benoit's had any more of those adorable gogo chicks come in. I wouldn't mind taking one of those home."

"Absolutely not," Henny said firmly. "Last thing we need is gogo guano dive-bombing the shop."

"What's a gogo?" I asked Esme.

"Let's go in dear, and you can see for yourself."

As soon as the door opened, a cacophony of animal sounds hit me. Squawks, chirps, growls, hisses, purrs, burbles, and mews erupted from a multitude of cages and separate areas cordoned-off by sturdy waist-high fences. The heavy scent of musty animal filled the room, the freshness of wood pine shavings, the nuttiness of seeds and feeders, all combined with the thick dampness of spilled water dishes. I spun around, trying to take it all in at once.

A cluster of rabbits roamed one of the enclosures. I stepped closer, leaning over the fence to get a good look.

Henny pulled me back. "Watch yourself."

"Were-rabbits," Benoit said from behind me. He must have heard us come in. "Fairly docile most of the time, but they enjoy an occasional nip as the moon waxes unto its full glory."

Erebus jumped off the ledge and rubbed against my leg. I bent down at ran my hand along his fur, being more careful as I moved to the feathered wings tucked tightly against his body.

"We saw Erebus at the Drip & Tipple," I said.

"Monsieur Erebus is a free spirit, darling. He merely deigns us with his presence, but always on his terms."

"Have you got any more of those precious gogo chicks?" Esme asked.

Benoit shook his head. "I'm afraid not, Miss Meriweather. The little cherubs were so popular."

No gogo guano for us, I guess.

"That's not why we're here, anyway," Henny said. "We need to scrape your salamanders."

Revulsion overtook Benoit's face. "Pardon? You wish to *scrape* my salamanders?"

"That's right," Henny said. "We're here for the slime. Need it for a recipe and we're all out."

"We're willing to pay, of course," Esme said. "We don't want to intrude, but it's urgent."

Benoit rubbed at his chin and glanced toward the back of his shop. "Sadly, I have only one precious salamander remaining. They are simply *impossible* to get ahold of at the moment." He clutched dramatically at his cravat. "Prices are *astronomical*."

"Don't try that game with us," Henny said. "We know the going price."

"In all fairness," Esme said meekly, "the going price is astronomical."

Henny shot her a glare.

Benoit laid one hand over the other and leaned heavily on his cane. "As keen as I am to assist in your endeavor, *scraping* my salamander—"

"Mr. Benoit, sir," I said in my most pleasant and pleading voice, "it's for my studies. You see, we've just had a meeting with the American Association of Potion Masters Youth Internship Program Compliance Officer and unless we can scrape your salamander, I may be forced to return to the orphanage."

The indifference on his face faltered. "The orphanage?"

"That's right, Benoit," Henny said. "She'll have to go back to those despicable conditions. Can you live with that on your conscience?"

Esme clutched my shoulders. "You could be her savior, and we'd be forever grateful."

The worry in his eyes met mine. I beamed back, eyelashes batting helplessly. "I wish I'd had a chance to see the gogos…"

His cravat quivered as he released an audible gasp. "Perhaps a few gentle grazes would be acceptable." He stamped his cane gently on the floor. "It would be an *absolute tragedy* if Carmody left us too soon. She simply cannot miss the gogos. Wait here and I will fetch the salamander."

As Benoit disappeared into the back of the store, the three of us heaved a sigh of relief.

"Good thinking," Henny said to me. "Benoit's a big softy. You hit him where it hurt."

"It's true. If we don't figure out who killed Oliver, I may have to go back to Ms. Ruthie, and that's the last thing I want."

Esme patted my arm. "We won't let that happen, dear."

A few moments later, Benoit emerged from the back with a small box with glass sides, covered with a light-weight cloth. He set the box on a nearby table and we crowded around.

"This is Mademoiselle Marguerite. She's a protected species and is extremely shy, so no sudden movements." He peeled off the cloth.

A tiny salamander huddled in one corner. Smooth, moist shiny yellow skin glistened under the harsh lights of the shop. Deep black speckles dotting her body from blunt snout to the tip of her tail.

"Hello Marguerite," I whispered.

She twitched, which I took as a positive acknowledgment.

"Be gentle," Benoit said. "She is a sensitive soul. What instrument are you employing to, uh, scrape her?"

Esme dug into a pocket in her skirt and pulled out a wooden-handled cotton swab and accompanying collection cup.

"Esme's got a knack for these types of things," Henny said. "Marguerite may enjoy it. Like a lizard back rub."

"Amphibian," Benoit corrected.

"I assure you," Esme said, "I've got a deft hand and a calming touch. She'll barely feel a thing. Watch closely, Carmody. Collecting ingredients from the environment may be a tad advanced for your level, but the opportunity to learn is here, so take note."

I stepped closer to watch Esme work. True to her words, she painted the swab across Marguerite's slimy skin with the delicacy of a fine artist. The salamander barely moved. In fact, she may have leaned in. Back rub indeed.

"Will it be enough?" I asked.

Esme held the swab up to the light and squinted at the sample. "It should be, but we don't want to waste it." The swab quickly disappeared into the collection cup and vanished into her pocket.

I whispered my thanks to Marguerite before Benoit covered her box with the cloth.

"You're a peach, Benoit." Henny slapped him on the shoulder. "You don't happen to own a trench coat, do you?"

He fumbled the box but quickly regained control and peeked under the cloth to check on Marguerite. "A trench coat, you ask?" He scoffed at the idea. "Certainly not. How utterly inelegant."

"Just checking," Henny said.

I said goodbye to the other animals as we left the shop, sample in hand. "Now we make the Untruth Serum?"

"Should be quick," Henny said. "Then off to Astrid's to put it to work."

"Will she even take it?" Esme asked. "We can't force her."

Henny grunted. "If she wants to keep her nose clean she will. And if she won't, well, then we'll know right quick who's to blame for Oliver."

"I'm not sure that's how it works," I said. But

excitement grew inside me at the thought of returning to the Dreamnasium. Of course, I was curious as to what Astrid knew—or didn't know—but even more curious to learn more about dream delving. What could she see? What could she see in me?

Thirteen

WITH A SINGLE tiny vial of carefully concocted Untruth Serum in hand, we entered the Dreamnasium through the front entrance, avoiding the alleyway, much to my relief.

Like before, the gentle tinkle of the door chime announced our arrival and Astrid emerged from the back a moment later in a gauzy, flowy dress that changed color in the light with every swish and step.

"Ah, Meriweathers. I've been expecting you."

"You—" Henny blinked away her surprise. "You're expecting us?"

Astrid gave her a sly smile. "Of course. Let's retreat to the Dreamnasium, and I'll be happy to take your potion."

Esme and Henny's faces went white, and I choked back a gurgle of surprise. *What did this woman know? How?*

"Follow me." Astrid turned with a flourish of her dress and dipped behind the darkened curtain.

I followed in her wake, with Henny and Esme following behind me with reluctant steps.

My face lit up with a broad smile as we entered into the open space of the Dreamnasium. I stared at the domed ceiling above in wonder. The hexagonal panes of swirling colored glass shined above and the pinpricks of a sky full of stars twinkled back.

Astrid led us to a seating area in the very center of the room. The chaise and lone velvet chair I'd seen the first time were still there, now joined by two more chairs. *She really was expecting us.*

"How did you know we were coming?" I asked.

Astrid gave me a knowing smile. "Would you believe I saw it in a dream?"

I nodded, mesmerized.

"Don't put fancy ideas in her head," Henny said. "I'm sure there's a perfectly good explanation."

"Like what?" Esme asked, bewildered.

"Like… Like she spotted us coming down the street."

"What about the potion?" Esme asked Henny.

Henny waved her hands wildly. "For heaven's sake Esme, we're always carrying potions. It's not hard to put that together."

Astrid observed this with a twitch of amusement at the corner of her mouth. Despite Henny's flailing, the only explanation that made any sense was that Astrid had indeed dreamed about our arrival.

"Once you two are finished, we can begin. I have one condition."

"What's that?" Henny demanded.

"You let Carmody sit for a delving."

Both twins physically recoiled.

"Absolutely not," Esme said and the same time

Henny sputtered, "Impossible."

Astrid clasped her hands calmly in front of her and waited.

"What are you trying to weasel out of her?" Henny asked with suspicion.

"Or put what strange ideas into her head?" Esme added.

"She clearly wants this experience. I've known since she first visited, isn't that right, Carmody?" Astrid turned to me for an answer.

I gulped back the guilt that rose in the back of my throat. "It sounds very…interesting."

"No, no, there's no way." Henny moved to grab my arm, but I turned away.

"I want to try it," I said. "I don't know any secrets. I have nothing to hide. Please let me try it once. I'd never get this experience at the orphanage."

The twins' protests stopped at mention of the orphanage. A dose of their own medicine seemed to shut them up just like it had affected Benoit.

"I don't want anyone to think we're denying you unique experiences," Esme said, "but are you sure you want to let someone into your head? It could be dangerous."

"Disastrous," Henny added.

"Or," Astrid cut in with a melodious voice, "it could be wonderful. Enlightening, refreshing." She looked at me. "Cathartic."

I'd read widely enough to know what those words meant. But cathartic? What did she mean by that?

"Take your place on the chaise," the dreamweaver said.

I did as Astrid instructed, easing myself onto the sofa. It was comfortable, with deep, plush cushions, and I melted into their warm hug.

"Would you like them to stay?" Astrid asked me, nodding toward Henny and Esme. "I'll need your consent. Delving is a private matter."

Despite my eagerness, a twinge of fear rose within me. Trepidation. "Yes, please let them stay."

Esme's eyes softened at my request and she smiled reassuringly. She and Henny sat in the two remaining chairs, hunching together, uncomfortable, arms squarely in their laps.

"As you wish." Astrid's voice was calm and slow, and she spoke in a hypnotic cadence. "Gaze up at the dome, Carmody Greene. You are floating within the universe. Let the stars take you across the skies."

I let my head rest on the pillow and stared at the twinkling blips of light flittering across the colorful dome. Some felt brighter, and constellations I'd missed before became clear. There was Orion and his three-starred belt. The Big Dipper.

"Your eyes are heavy," Astrid's voice droned melodiously. "So heavy. It is soothing to close your eyes. Rest your eyes."

The stars blinked out and, to my great relief, an aching behind my eyes I hadn't known was there drifted away on Astrid's words.

"You are floating among the endless stars. You can fly. Where will you fly, Carmody?"

My breathing was low and steady. "Away."

"Away from where?"

"From who."

"Away from who?"

"Ms. Ruthie," I hear myself say. The weight of my body was so heavy, as though I were granite, unmovable. My eyes were the weight of boulders. I could do nothing but keep them shut. I felt this in myself, I was aware, but not aware, the way one feels as they wake from a dream, knowing they are dreaming but still not awake.

"You leave Ms. Ruthie behind. She disappears to a pinprick in the distance. Where will you go, Carmody?"

In my mind, Ms. Ruthie rushes backward, away from me, at enormous speed until she is nothing but a dot in the sky. "I go to the potion shop. It is lovely. The twins welcome me and we laugh and make potions. I am able to tingle effortlessly. I am a natural talent."

"You are with the Meriweather twins. You are happy. Where do you go now, Carmody?"

Our laughter dies down. "I go to the alleyway. I see Oliver laying crumpled beneath the dumpster, hidden by a burlap cloth."

A voice not of my dream intrudes. "I must insist you stop this, Astrid. She's clearly—"

Oliver rises slowly from beneath the burlap. It slides off his thin body and pools on the cobbles. A bony arm raises and points behind me. I turn to look. The silhouette of a figure stands at the mouth of the alley. There is something strange about the shape.

I turn back to Oliver. Hollow eyes stare through me.

My fingers burn.

I scream.

"You are floating among the stars. You feel light as your eyes flutter open."

As if compelled, my eyes blinked open.

"You are back among us, Carmody." Astrid placed a hand behind my shoulder and eased me into a sitting position. My legs dangled over the edge.

The twins rushed to my side.

"Are you all right, dear?" Esme cupped my face in her hands. "Are you hurt?"

I held my hands in my lap until the familiar burning subsided. "I'm fine. I'm okay."

Henny chewed rocks. "This dreamweaving is... Well, it's no good, Astrid."

I glanced at Astrid, but her face was unreadable. There were no furrows in her brow, no raised eyebrows or other indication of a reaction.

After a long pause, Astrid said, "She is a strong dreamwalker."

"She is nothing of the sort," Henny barked. "Don't even start. If you think you're going to purloin our intern, think again. Find your own." She swooped a protective arm around me and hoisted me up from the chaise onto unsteady legs. "We should have never agreed to this mystical jiggery-pokery."

The dreamweaver stood by with an amused look on her face as Henny dropped me into one of the nearby chairs. Esme kneeled by my side and checked me over, as though what I'd just seen would somehow manifest on the outside. Wooziness overtook me and I drooped, draping myself over the side of the chair for support.

"It was Oliver," I said weakly. "He was trying to show me something."

"Oliver?" Henny choked. "That's just the delirium talking. Some residual of Astrid's silly ritual, no doubt."

"Certainly not." Astrid voice was clear and calm.

"She saw what the universe wanted her to see."

"Well *the universe* can mind its own business and stay out of Carmody's head."

"Could you see what I saw?" I asked the dream-weaver.

She nodded slowly. "That's part of the connection."

Henny grumbled through her teeth words I could not make out, then pointed to Astrid with a barbed finger. "Carmody's suffered through her part, now it's your part of the bargain."

Astrid splayed out her hands. "As promised."

Esme fished in her pockets for the precious vial of Untruth Serum. "You know what this is?"

A sly smile crossed Astrid's face. "Of course. As I said, I have seen it. Since I cannot share my clients' information, you have to go about this indirectly."

Esme nodded. "Correct. You will only be able to speak in lies. Once you swallow this, it will take effect immediately. Are you ready?"

Astrid nodded, then took the vial from Esme and downed the contents in one gulp. A moment later, an even deeper calmness fell behind her eyes. She was in a trance. She'd gone docile.

Henny pushed forward, stepping up to Astrid so their faces were inches apart.

"Astrid Starcaller, do you answer these questions freely?"

"No."

"Good. Astrid Starcaller, what is your profession?"

"I am a baker."

Henny snorted, but continued, "Astrid Starcaller, who is the mayor of this town?"

"Peter Furlap."

"God save us from that nightmare," Henny muttered.

"Keep going and stop testing her," Esme urged. "That small dose won't last long."

"Astrid Starcaller, were you in the alleyway next to this shop the day Oliver Oliphant was killed, yes or no?"

"No."

Henny and Esme exchanged glances. I held my breath, and the anticipation threatened to suffocate me.

"Astrid Starcaller, did you kill Oliver Oliphant?"

We waited what seemed an eternity.

Finally, she answered. "Yes."

The balloon of suspense deflated and the weight of expectation lifted from my shoulders. I let in a deep breath. Astrid wasn't the killer.

"Astrid Starcaller, did you see anything suspicious the day Oliver Oliphant was murdered?"

"Yes."

"Darn." Henny slapped a thigh.

My energy had returned, and I felt strong enough to stand up. After listening to Henny, I thought I had the hang of this questioning thing. "Let's try a different approach. Astrid Starcaller, did Oliver visit you the day he was killed?"

"No."

Esme clutched Henny's arm. "He *was* here."

"Astrid Starcaller," I continued, "was Oliver Oliphant here for a dream delve?"

"No."

Now we were getting somewhere.

"Astrid Starcaller, was Oliver Oliphant's delve about the mayor's race?"

"Yes."

"Astrid Starcaller, was Oliver Oliphant's delve about his job as Regulations and Town Standards Chief Inspector?"

"Yes."

I turned to Esme and Henny. "I thought that might be it, but I guess not. Any ideas?"

Henny grimaced. "I don't want to ask if it was about his love life."

Esme shrugged helplessly. "No idea. This backwards questioning has me turned upside down."

Astrid leaned against the dream delving table, calm as a clam, eyes hazy waiting for our next question.

"She's getting comfortable," Esme said. "That's a bad sign. The potion's effects won't last forever."

I struggled to find a path without direct questioning. We'd be asking forever covering all the negative space of things that *didn't* happen. Then I remembered what Astrid had said about seeing what her clients saw.

"Astrid Starcaller, was Oliver Oliphant here to get answers to a question?"

"No."

Bingo.

"Astrid Starcaller, did you see something Oliver Oliphant didn't want you to see in his dream?"

"No."

Double bingo.

"Keep going," Henny said to me.

My own vision of Oliver came to mind. He was pointing at someone, but who? "Astrid Starcaller, did you see Oliver with another person?"

"No."

"Astrid Starcaller, did you know this other person?"

"I could see the other person clearly."

I blinked. *What?*

Esme tapped me on the shoulder. "You asked her a question she couldn't answer. She's lying for clarity. She didn't see the person clearly, so she doesn't know if she knows them or not."

"Got it. Let me try again." I turned back to the dream-weaver. She continued to lean casually against the table, waiting for my next question, but her eyes were now more focused than hazy. "Astrid Starcaller, did Oliver Oliphant seem secretive about this other person?"

Astrid stared at me a moment and tilted her head as if confused. "No."

"The potion's wearing off," Esme said.

"Astrid Starcaller, do you know what Oliver Oli-phant and this person were discussing?"

"No."

My words ran quickly, trying to stuff in another ques-tion before the potion wore off completely. I wasn't thinking, I was just trying to get answers. "Astrid Starcaller, what were they discussing?"

"Turtles."

"Turtles?" I repeated.

Astrid's eyes inspected me with suspicious curiosity. "What about turtles?"

"It's over," Esme said with a sigh. "She's out of the trance."

Astrid checked herself over, but seemed satisfied that everything was still as it should be. "Well, I hope you got what you came for."

"And you won't tell us any more of what you saw?"

Henny asked. "Even though you know it might be important?"

"Miss Meriweather, as a member of a professional organization yourself, I'm sure you understand the confidentiality of the dreamweaver and client covenant. Under the Dreamweaver's Association laws I cannot speak of my clients *directly*. My hands are tied unless subpoenaed by a court and authorized by the Association. This serum of yours was a masterful idea, I must say. I'd be happy to answer more questions *untruthfully* if you have more."

I frowned. Marguerite had been scraped dry. "That's impossible."

"Too bad," Astrid said. "But if you ever want to come around and delve again, you're more than welcome. Your dreams are very clear. You have a real talent."

"Even without the star mark?"

Astrid shrugged. "Are you sure you don't have one?"

I mentally inspected my body, but I was pretty sure I'd have noticed.

Henny waved Astrid off. "Stop trying to steal our intern. She's got a talent for the tingle, so enough of this star mark business. We got what we came for, pitiful as it was, and now we're leaving. Esme, let's go." Henny quickly shuffled me from the Dreamnasium through the lobby and onto the street.

The bright daylight made me squint. "I don't think it was a total loss," I said to the twins. "We know Oliver had been or was going to meet someone and that Oliver seemed secretive about their meetings."

"That doesn't tell us anything," Henny said.

Esme sighed. "I don't know what we're supposed to do with that information, Carmody. It doesn't lead us anywhere."

"We know that Oliver met with someone in the alleyway before he was murdered. We know that Oliver dreamed of meeting someone in the alleyway for secretive reasons. When I was with Astrid, Oliver pointed at a shadowy figure and I knew that person had something to do with Oliver's murder."

"Is that what you saw in your dream?" Esme asked.

"Yes." The memories of the dream delving ran through my mind. "And there's something else."

The twins leaned in closer.

"I felt an overwhelming sense of dread."

Fourteen

ROANNA SET DOWN our usual orders then straddled the backwards chair at our table. "I've told you guys I had nothing to do with Oliver."

"We know," Henny said. "That's not why we're here. We needed a drink after the day we've had."

"We've just come from the Dreamnasium," I said.

Roanna's mouth clapped closed.

"Astrid didn't spill the beans on you," Henny said. "Don't worry."

"Then what *did* she tell you?"

"We know Oliver was at the Dreamnasium that day."

The bartender bit her lower lip. "I should have told you that. He was pressing Astrid for a discount on his delve when I got there."

"Sounds about right," Henny said with a derisive sniff. "Always on the prowl for some way to exploit his position."

Exploit his position... I thought back to my vision at the Dreamnasium and considered what I knew of Oliver. Pointed, vindictive, egotistical. Not exactly the type of person to cower from anyone. Whatever happened in that alleyway, it was at Oliver's choosing. "What if Oliver was meeting someone for a deal? To exploit his position, like you said."

Esme took a dainty sip from her tea. "What kind of deal, dear?"

"Well, he was trying to skim from Astrid, and Henny makes it sound like that's not out of the ordinary. It could be anything."

"*Anything* is the operative word," Henny said. "It could have been about his seedy election campaign for all we know."

"How is election talk alleyway material?" I asked.

Henny took a heavy swig from her whiskey. "Ever heard of bribes? Backroom deals? Lobbyists?"

Roanna smirked. "I doubt we have anything to fear from the dreaded Chester Hollow lobbyists. But now that you mention it, Theo's been making more enemies than frenemies lately. Maybe she thinks she's got the election in the bag now that Oliver's gone."

"What enemies?" I asked.

She nodded to a table on the tearoom side of the pub. A sour-faced woman in a frilled, high-neck blouse sat upright in one of the chairs, alone, staring coldly into her drink. "Prudence just got fired from Town Hall. She might be willing to spill some tea, if you ask the right questions."

"No Untruth Serum needed, thankfully," Esme said. "Prudence should tell us everything with only gentle prodding. Last month I ran into her at the bookstore and without prompting she told me all about her neighbor's hemorrhoids and her supervisor's addiction to a certain brand of gin."

Henny let out a hoot. "Maybe *that's* why she got fired."

"It wasn't the supervisor," Roanna said. "It was definitely Theo. Prudence told me herself, along with how Max Martins asked old Mrs. Travers' daughter out on a date last week, but she said no so he asked Rebecca Skint instead, but I guess Rebecca was busy so he eventually ended up going out with Trina Bellows."

My head spun.

Roanna jabbed a thumb toward the bar. "Gotta get back. Let me know what you learn from Prudence." She hopped up and headed toward the counter, but spun back. "And find out if Trina's on for a second date with Max."

Henny grabbed her whiskey. "Let's go."

We scooped up our respective drinks and followed her to Prudence's table, taking the three remaining seats. The woman's face barely changed as we sat.

"Hello Prudence," Henny said. "Word on the street is you got fired from Town Hall."

Prudence's sour mouth puckered even more. "It's shameful. Retaliatory, even. How much have you heard?"

"Just that Theo gave you the heave-ho," Henny said. "We were hoping you could give us the full debrief."

Esme's teacup settled on its saucer with a tinkle. "And we're supposed to ask if Trina Bellows and Max Martins are on for a second date."

Henny's own face puckered. "Give us the skinny on you and Theo first. Trina can wait."

Prudence took a sip of her beverage and cleared her throat, then she set her elbows on the table and leaned in, prompting us to lean in as well. "Well, earlier today, I was minding my own business working on the contract for the town's street cleaning services when Theo happened to walk by my cubicle. Now, I don't normally like to stop and chat. I'm a very reserved person and mostly keep to myself, but today I noticed that the mayor was looking particularly agitated and, honestly, haggard—circles under her eyes, bits of hair sticking out in all directions, that sort of thing." Prudence put a hand to her chest. "I'm certainly not the type to point out flaws in peoples' appearances, but I thought it best to say something in case Mayor Theo was headed to an event and wanted to freshen up her look, if you get my meaning."

"You were probably doing her a favor," I said. *An unsolicited favor.*

Prudence tutted. "You'd think. But imagine my surprise when, after I'd politely told the mayor she looked terrible, she rounded on me like a viper. I thought she would bite my head right off."

"What did she say to you?" I asked.

"Nothing kind, I assure you that. I tried to calm her down. I told her I was only trying to help and that she'd looked a mess off and on ever since she had all that equipment moved into her office."

Our eyes narrowed in unison.

"What equipment?" Henny asked.

Prudence shook her head as if it weren't important. "Some glass cases or something. I don't know what she's trying to show off, but she seemed really secretive about it, which is contradictory, don't you think? Anyway, I only caught a glimpse because I was tucked out of sight behind one of the big pillars in the hallways waiting for Marybeth Simmons because we always get our coffee together and—"

"How big were the cases?" I asked.

Henny and Esme looked at me questioningly.

"I can hardly remember." Prudence held up her hands and stretched them about two feet apart. "Maybe about yea big. Probably to hold awards or trophies or something gaudy."

I turned to Henny and Esme. "The same as we saw Wee Harv carrying the other day."

The twins leaned back deeply into their chairs and let it sink in.

Prudence set down her cup with a thud. "Do you even *care* about my situation or are you fixated on the mayor's display cases?"

"Sorry, dear," Esme said. "Please continue."

"So, I show up to work today, ready to do my part, serve the public, greater good and all that, and what do I find on my desk? A notice that my employment has been terminated."

"Did they give a reason?" I asked.

At this, Prudence's pucker took a dour turn. "Misuse of township property. That's all it said."

"Any idea what they meant by that?" I asked.

Prudence scoffed. "I assume it's a cover story. The worst I've ever done was borrow a stapler over the weekend. I'm a model employee. No demerits, exceptional performance evaluations. I can only assume Theo didn't appreciate my comments about how she looked and decided personal vendettas were more important than serving the interests of the public."

"That does sound like our mayor." Esme nodded slowly while taking a dainty sip of tea.

"Rotten to the core," Henny said.

"Of course, you know how horrible she can be, Henny. Why, that fight of yours—"

Henny leaned forward and wagged a finger toward Prudence. "I was goaded into that fight, you know. Goaded."

"What will you do now?" I asked Prudence.

"I suppose I'll give Astrid a visit. She can show me what would be most beneficial."

"She can do that?" I asked. "Tell the future?"

"She's no fortune teller," Henny said with a snap. "Don't get ideas."

"I'm out of a job," Prudence said, "so Astrid's my best bet. And I'll tell you one thing, she's worth the money." She tipped her head back and down the remainder of her tea in one dramatic gulp. "I've got to catch her before she closes. Good evening, Meriweathers." She rose from her chair and nodded my way. "You too, whoever you are."

"Our intern," Henny and Esme said in unison.

As Prudence disappeared through the pub door, Esme gave a start. "Oh dear. We didn't find out if Trina was going on a second date with Max."

* * *

I left the Drip & Tipple with more questions than answers. What did Mayor Theo want with a glass case? Maybe it *was* to put her awards and accolades on display, but that didn't explain the secretive nature Prudence had described, or the way Theo unceremoniously terminated her employment on shaky grounds—assuming Prudence's tale was accurate in the first place.

"Well, well, well," Henny said. "Speak of the devil."

I followed Henny's gaze and spotted Theo straightening a sign outside a shop window a few doors down from the Drip & Tipple.

"We should be cautious," Esme said. "We don't want her to see us. I hate when she asks us questions."

"Hey, Theo!" Henny shouted.

Esme groaned.

Theo turned, saw who it was, then grimaced and returned to her task.

I could hardly keep up with Henny's long, determined strides down the sidewalk as she made a beeline toward the mayor.

Once close enough, I saw that the sign Theo had been straightening was her own election banner. It boasted a heavily doctored photograph of Theo with a gleaming white politician's smile accompanied by the words "Vote Papadopoulos. Help her help you."

Although we stood right next to her, Mayor Theo did not immediately acknowledge us. Instead, she took an inordinate amount of time straightening the poster to the millimeter before finally turning to us. "Yes?"

"Exactly the person we wanted to see." Henny's grin was obnoxiously wide.

"Is that so?"

"Sure, sure," Henny said. "We just spoke with poor, unemployed Prudence."

She murmured, "Mm." Theo wasn't taking the bait.

"Care to share your side of the story?" Henny asked.

Theo clasped her hands demurely in front of her. "Township personnel matters are confidential."

"New poster," Esme cut in. "It looks nice."

Theo rounded on Esme as if she'd just appeared. "Thank you." She admired the poster once more. "It really captures my likeness, don't you think?"

"Yes," I said. "It should really make a difference. How are the polls going?"

"Excellent, considering I'm running uncontested."

"How convenient," Henny said with a sneer. "No more Oliver means no more competition."

Theo ran her hands along the poster once again, straightening out the wrinkles. "I have nothing to hide regarding Oliver. He was my— He was the *town's* top income driver. Besides, there's no chance I'd lose an election to Oliver. You know as well as I do that everyone hated him. He relished in it, but it was no way to win over the people. Honestly, I don't know why he thought to run in the first place."

"Probably sick of the current regime like the rest of us," Henny said.

"If you're tired of your current mayor, you could always run yourself, Henrietta Meriweather."

"Oh dear," Esme mumbled. "Don't give her ideas."

Henny stabbed a pointed finger toward Theo. "I just might."

Theo appeared unperturbed by the knobby digit directed at her chest, Instead, she took a few steps down the sidewalk and began to fuss with another campaign poster. "Please do, Henny. It would make my day." A devious grin spread across her face. I wasn't sure how much more popular Henny would be with her jagged, rough edges compared to Theo's slick and polished facade.

"Can you tell us about the glass cases in your office?"

I asked, trying to steer the conversation back to the reason we were talking to the mayor in the first place.

"Glass cases?" Theo repeated my words as if confused. "I'm not sure what you mean."

"Don't try that act with us," Henny said.

"Prudence mentioned you had a number of large glass cases delivered," Esme said. "We were just curious what they were for."

"What they were for is none of your business."

"Would it be our business to ask what you were asking Constable Potts to dispose of for you the night of the gala?" I surprised myself with my boldness. This was the mayor I was pressing!

Theo's eyes narrowed to the smallest of slits. "What are you talking about?"

"Bit of backroom dealing, eh, Theo?" Henny rubbed her hands together.

Theo's lips pursed into a tight line. "I don't know what you think you think you know, but you don't know."

Esme blinked in confusion. "Pardon?"

The polish slipped from Theo's voice. "I mean stop poking around where your nose doesn't belong."

"We know you got these cases delivered from Big Harv. Special order?" I didn't expect an answer. "And we know you gave Constable Potts something secretive to get rid of. And now Prudence says the glass cases are nowhere to be seen."

Theo eyed me with disdain, but I held my stare.

Finally, she broke. "Fine," she said. "I had glass cases delivered. So what? Glass cases aren't illegal."

I continued to hold my stare. "What were the cases for?"

Theo's face pinched. "My salamanders."

"Salamanders?" Esme appeared more confused than ever. "Why would you want salamanders in your office?"

The mayor let out a groan and a sigh. "It doesn't matter because they weren't even salamanders."

"Explain," Henny demanded.

"I purchased a breeding pair of extremely rare salamanders from a man who promised me they'd be an absolute gold mine. There's a salamander shortage, apparently."

Esme nodded. "The prices have skyrocketed, and Benoit's only got Marguerite at the menagerie."

"What man?" I asked, getting back to Theo.

"I don't know who he was. He was all shadowy. Didn't talk much. Hid his face and wore a trench coat."

I exchanged stern looks with Henny and Esme.

"Anyway," Theo continued, "I brought them back and got the case set up in my back office, but I realized pretty quickly that something was wrong."

"Like what?" Henny's voice held a skeptical note.

"The slime trails, for one. And they didn't walk with their little legs, just skooched along on their bellies up and down the glass walls. I took a real close look then, and wouldn't you know it, the shady guy in a trench coat had sold me banana slugs."

"Banana slugs with little arms?" I asked.

Esme nodded solemnly. "It must have been some variant of a protuberance potion, a mid-level gel recipe that grows appendages. It's highly regulated, though, and didn't come from us. You can imagine what unscrupulous individuals would do with something like that."

"Like grow fake legs onto banana slugs," I said.

Esme averted her eyes. "Worse, I'm afraid."

"Imagine *my* surprise," Theo said, "but I had to get rid of them. They were no use and if Benoit found out I'd even planned to breed salamanders, well, it wouldn't be good for the campaign. He's the chapter president of B.A.R.F. you know."

"What's *B.A.R.F.*?" I asked.

"Basic Animal Rights Federation," Theo said. "He'd sick them on me in an instant. The slugs had to go."

Henny fell into merciless guffaws only stopping to grab at a stitch in her side. "So," she said through huffs, "let me get this straight. You bought what you thought were black market salamanders from a random stranger in an alleyway but they turned out to be regular old banana slugs with useless little legs?" She flapped her arms like overcooked noodles.

"Don't look at me like that," Theo hissed. "They could easily be confused with salamanders if you didn't look too close. They have the same slimy skin and markings. Yes, I was a fool. It was a mistake. It was supposed to be fast money."

"There's nothing fast about banana slugs." Henny doubled over, wheezing with laughter.

We had an explanation for Theo's odd behavior, but there was still one piece missing. Obviously, she couldn't have gone to Benoit's for the glass cases. "How'd you know where to get the cases?" I asked. "I wouldn't think Big Harv's Enchanted Imports & Antiques would be the obvious spot."

Theo shook her head dismissively. "The man in the trench coat told me."

* * *

The man in the trench coat. He kept popping up. And according to Mayor Theo, he was directing his clandestine clients to Big Harv's place for salamander supplies.

Theo had left us there to ponder what she'd said. I'm sure she thought sharing her secret would get us off her back, and in a way, it worked.

I watched as Henny ran a finger across the mayor's election poster. When she pulled away, a spindly black mustache graced Theo's perfectly airbrushed upper lip.

Henny held up a tiny jar and her grinned deepened. "I had some leftover Arthritis Antidote. Goes on real dark. Too bad we didn't have any of Maude's hairy salve. This would have been the perfect application."

My hand twitched toward the jar concealed in my pocket. Still there. Still hidden.

"Oh dear." Esme tutted and pulled a handkerchief from the depths of her sleeve and wiped off the graffiti. "We're already suspected of Oliver's murder. We don't need a charge of defacing property."

"Not defacing," Henny said. "An obvious improvement."

"What about the man in the trench coat?" I asked.

"What about him, dear? Do you think Oliver caught him selling banana slug salamanders?"

"Maybe," I said after a minute of thought. "Why do you think he'd send Theo to Big Harv's?"

"Business kickbacks?" Henny offered.

"I think we should ask Big Harv. We know he was stockpiling glass cases, and what antique furniture dealer needs a hundred glass cases if you don't have a plan to sell them?"

Henny frowned. "He must have been in on the scam all along. Sounds like Big Harv to a T. It's those burl wood bowls all over again."

"But this time someone is dead," I said.

Esme let out a squeak. "If Big Harv was part of a scam, shouldn't we get Constable Potts?"

"Esme," Henny said, "Constable Potts disposed of Theo's salamander—banana slugs—whatever. He's part of the problem. And I'll remind you he thinks we're guilty, and we were told not to investigate or interfere."

Each reason Henny spouted off deepened the look of concern on Esme's face. "Then what can we do?" she asked.

"We don't know for sure that Big Harv did anything wrong," I said. "A few questions can't hurt."

"I don't know, Carmody," Esme said. "Maybe we should get back to your lessons. The compliance officer made it very clear that you have exceptional potion-making abilities and we should foster that, right Henny? Henny?"

"Eh?" Henny grunted.

"Carmody's lessons?"

"Lessons? Oh, yes. We should get on that." Henny took two long strides down the sidewalk. "Right after a trip to Big Harv's."

Fifteen

I COULD HAVE heard a pin drop as we entered Big Harv's Enchanted Imports & Antiques. The only movement in the place were the dust motes floating through the stuffy air.

"Looks like nobody's home," Esme said.

"Big Harv!" Henny called out. "Show yourself."

Nothing.

"Maybe they're in the back," I said.

"We should come back later," Esme said. "Perhaps after Carmody's lessons are complete."

"Shh." Henny waggled her hand to quiet us down. "I thought I heard something."

I listened intently, but it was only us and the dust motes, and they made no sound.

"Let's poke around," Henny said.

We weaved our way through the trail of furniture. Items stacked upon items threatened to topple and bury us like a rock slide. Ahead, the magical armoire was still in its place, looming slightly crooked at the end of the main pathway. I'd have been scared to move it too if it had eaten me once before. At least no mumbles emanated from a victim trapped inside this time.

"I guess we're out of luck," Henny said.

"Wait." I angled my ears toward a faint sound I'd just heard. "There *is* someone here."

"Are you sure, dear?" Esme looked around at the cavern of sideboards and side chairs. "We might as well go back—"

"Darn it, Wee!" Big Harv's growl came from the depths of the warehouse. "To the right, not left. Right!"

Henny quickly brought a finger to her lips.

We tip-toed through the meandering paths toward the area of the shop where I'd spotted Wee Harv the first time. A set of heavy black curtains now shielded our view.

Splitting the curtain an inch, we peeked through. Big Harv stood on a raised metal platform overlooking a large, open receiving area. A set of stairs led up to the platform from a spot to our right. A tall rolling service door took up most of the far wall, opened just enough for a light breeze to waft through the space.

Wee Harv was hard at work stacking glass cases along the wall opposite Big Harv. The tiny man pointed and shouted commands, and Wee Harv would lumber along with the directions.

"Tall ones to the left, I said. Left!" Big Harv's face was as red as Ms. Ruthie's favorite lipstick. He stamped his feet on the platform each time Wee Harv placed a case even an inch out of place.

"We don't have all day," he yelled. "I need these stacked and ready to offload by tonight, so hurry up."

I tapped Henny and Esme on their shoulders and they

turned to me. I kept my voice low. "All these glass cases, Big Harv was definitely aware of the salamander scheme. He was ready to supply all these enclosures for the fake salamanders. There's no other reason I can think of why he'd stock up on so many."

"But it sounds like he's trying to get rid of them," Esme said. "He just said he's offloading them tonight."

That was strange. Had a deal gone bad? Was someone on his tail? I shook my head and nearly laughed aloud at myself. *We* were on his tail.

Esme leaned in closer. "And what does any of it have to do with Oliver?"

"Let's ask." Henny swiped aside the curtain and strode into the open before I could stop her.

Big Harv stopped mid-sentence, clearly shocked at Henny's sudden arrival. "What the blazes are you doing here?" His eyes flitted to the stacks. He waved a hand for Wee Harv to cover them up and the big man struggled, hastily tossing a drop cloth over the pile.

"We've got some questions, Harv. Come on down from there."

Big Harv didn't budge. "Can't you see we're busy? And this area is off limits to the public."

I stepped forward, revealing myself from behind the curtain. "Why's that?"

"You too?" His glower grew deeper as Esme appeared beside me.

"What are all these cases for?" I asked.

"That's none of your business, young lady."

"Got any mutated banana slugs slithering around?" Henny raised an eyebrow and made a show of scanning the cavernous space.

At this, Big Harv's face grew dark. A bass "Uh" emanated from his gigantic son.

"Quiet, Wee," Big Harv seethed. He rounded on Henny. "I don't know what you think you're getting at, but business is business. So, show yourselves out."

Having entered the larger space, I gave it a good look. Besides the odd table or sideboard, a string of wooden chairs, linked together by a strong cable were suspended from the ceiling and ran the length of the back room, disappearing into the main warehouse space. Then one thing caught my eye. Draped on the spindle at the bottom of the metal staircase leading to Big Harv's perch was a dark trench coat. Its extended length pooled on the floor, reminding me of the puddle of Oliver snugged under a burlap cloth in that alleyway.

I tapped Henny and Esme on the shoulder and pointed to the trench coat.

Henny's eyes narrowed, and she turned back to Big Harv. "Well, well. Playing all sides of the deal, I see."

Big Harv froze.

Henny clasped her hands together and smiled. "I'm pretty sure our dearly departed Oliver was spotted talking to a man in a trench coat not too long before he was murdered."

A moment passed. Suddenly, Big Harv shouted, "Run, Wee!" before sprinting the length of the metal platform, his tiny legs a blur. He leaped onto the string of cabled wooden chairs. He barely managed to grab a hold of the first chair's stretcher bar, then swung his way to the next chair just like I used to traverse the park's monkey bars near the orphanage as a kid.

At the same time, Wee Harv lumbered toward the

large rolled-up door. He ducked down low and scrambled through the opening, but it wasn't quite open enough. His bulk caught on the door, pinning him against the floor. Two legs the size of tree trunks waved helplessly as he tried to free himself.

Henny rushed over, the heavy footfalls of her boots echoing throughout the warehouse. She grabbed one of Wee Harv's flailing ankles and held fast. He wiggled and writhed, but Henny weathered the storm, dodging his other foot each time it swung in her direction. She used her own weight to keep the man's leg secure. "I've got this one," she shouted through labored breaths. "Catch Big Harv before he gets away."

"There he goes." Esme pointed high up toward the wily little man, who'd managed to make his way across four more chair lengths.

He was making too much progress. I followed the trajectory of the chair's cabled highway. It led from the back loading space over the wall of curtains and into the main showroom. He knew this maze better than we did. I couldn't let him get out of our sight or he'd disappear into the recesses of the forest of furniture. But how could we catch him? A solution sprung to mind.

"Chase after him, Esme. I've got an idea."

She blinked at me. "Chase…?" She lifted her head toward the raised platform and stared with wide-eyed trepidation.

Leaving Esme to face her fear, I threw the curtains aside and rushed into the other room. I shimmied through the narrow pathway, following the map etched in my memory of where to turn until I'd reached the moaning armoire. It loomed before me, grumbling. Looking up, I found the line of chairs and gauged their course. Just as I'd suspected, the chairs led almost directly under the armoire.

From the other room, I heard Henny shouting. "You can do it, Esme, one step at a time. Just don't look down."

I had to hurry before Esme lost her nerve. Rounding the armoire, I lined myself up with the chairs, then pushed the heavy piece of furniture inch-by-inch until it was in the right spot, ignoring its groans of displeasure. With a mighty heave, I pushed my shoulder against the bulky frame. It rocked a few times, but didn't overturn. I tried again, huffing with each diminishing push. My energy was failing.

I was too weak.

Too helpless.

Henny and Esme were giving all they could, and I was going to let them down. I'd return to the orphanage, defeated. Ms. Ruthie would scold me and I'd be on KP and bathroom duty until I aged out, then shipped off to Crazy Barry's Bargain Basement Brooms to take up my spot on the factory line, shriveling away until I died at an unnaturally young age.

My eyes narrowed. *No.*

I steeled myself, letting the memories of Ms. Ruthie's cruelty fade, replaced with the warmth, affection, and confidence the Meriweathers had given me. I was special. I had talent. And I was going to be a potion master just like them.

With a running start, I let out a primal scream as I leaped against the front of the armoire with all my strength, latching on with both hands with whatever flimsy grip I could snag. It rocked on its back legs, threatening to topple. I squeezed my eyes shut as the thing finally crashed onto its back with a cacophonous *whomp!*

Crawling off, I feared I'd smashed it to bits, but a hasty inspection proved otherwise. The armoire was in place and intact.

I didn't linger long savoring my effort because a cry carried from the loading room. I rushed back to check on Henny and Esme.

Henny still held fast onto Wee Harv's ankle, and it appeared the big man had finally been worn down enough that he'd stopped fighting back. Henny had that effect on people.

Poor Esme clung to the railing of the metal platform, frozen with eyes as wide as tea saucers. Each step must have been a monumental effort, but she was making pro-gress. Big Harv wouldn't be able to retreat that way. He could only monkey-bar his way forward. Right into my trap.

Sixteen

Big Harv's energy was waning. Each swing forward was more laborious than the last, but he spent a few moments each time to gather his breath before lunging for the next chair's stretcher bar. Despite the slow pace, his progress was steady, and he'd make enough ground that he finally passed from the loading room into the main showroom space. A few more chairs and he'd be right where I wanted him.

"What are you doing down there?" He twisted to look down toward where I laid in wait among the furniture. "Leave me alone!"

"Why are you running, then?" I shouted back. "Unless you have something to hide."

"Mind your business, young lady."

But I wasn't the one swinging along a tenuously threaded row of wooden chairs trying to escape.

There was one last piece to my plan that I hadn't accounted for. Looking around, all I saw were large, heavy pieces of furniture. Not a book or a table lamp or a paper weight to be found. Then I remembered what was hidden in my pocket, hastily stashed there earlier that morning. I pulled out the sample of Hair Apparent. I hefted it like a sturdy puck in my hand. Perfect.

He was almost directly over the armoire, but I waited until he'd committed to one more swing before throwing the latch and opening the armoire door directly beneath him. He panted, out of breath, and stared down at the yawning mouth.

The armoire's stomach growled. It was waiting to be fed.

"No, no, no." Big Harv scrambled to grab the next chair but one hand slipped off. His arm dangled in thin air before finally latching back onto the chair bar.

I gave the salve a little toss into the air, catching it in my palm, then chucked the thing directly at Big Harv's head. It was just like throwing pebbles at the birds perched on the power lines above Ms. Ruthie's freshly washed car.

The container exploded on impact. Goopy salve landed everywhere. His grip slipped momentarily, yet he held on with one desperate hand.

Drat.

But the salve wasn't finished. Hair suddenly sprouted from every spot it had landed—his face, his arms, his hands. A great mane of hair cascaded down his back, wafting in the cool air of the warehouse. And a single tiny drop had splattered on the chair's stretcher bar, right where Big Harv grabbed with his loose hand. Strands of glossy, flowy locks erupted between his fingers. Big Harv could not hold on.

"Ahh!" He slipped from the chair and fell right into the gaping maw of the hungry armoire.

As soon as he landed, I lifted the heavy door and let it slam into place.

He banged from the inside with both fists—"Lemme awt!"—but the magical locking handle held fast.

I cupped a hand to my ear. "What's that? Couldn't quite make out what you said." A satisfied grin spread across my face.

Heavy footfalls coming from the pathway caught my attention. A moment later, Henny and Esme appeared, starting at the fallen armoire, then at me with quizzical looks.

Another muffled demand and puny pounding emanated from behind the armoire's locked door.

"That complaining sounds just like Big Harv," Henny said. "Guess he never stops."

"Goodness, dear." Esme stared at the armoire in disbelief. "Did you catch him *in the wardrobe*?"

"What about Wee?" I asked Henny.

She jabbed a thumb toward the back warehouse. "He wiggled himself into a pretzel and eventually conked out. There's no way he's getting out from under that big door, anyway."

"We should call Constable Potts," Esme said.

"Now hang on a minute." Henny stepped up to the armoire and knocked twice on the wooden door. "You in there Harv?"

A grumpy and muffled "Yrs" was the response.

"Now, Big Harv," Henny said in a condescending tone, "if we open this thing, are you going to jump up and run away?"

"Jes urpin tha dur!"

"That didn't sound like a *no* to me." Henny

artificially raised her voice and addressed Esme and me. "What do you ladies think? Was that an affirmative? I'm not so sure. Oh well, I guess we leave him in here until the authorities arrive."

More vigorous pounding. "Nur, Nur. Ah won run!"

"Are you sure we should do this?" Esme whispered.

"Just block the pathway," Henny responded. "He's not going anywhere."

Esme turned to me. "What do you think, Carmody? You caught him, after all."

I couldn't imagine the tiny man scrambling his way from our net. The walls of furniture were high and Esme had blocked the main exit. Besides, I wanted answers. "Let's see what he has to say."

Henny grunted in approval and flicked the lock on the door and it sprung open. Big Harv, disheveled and still sporting an abundance of hair sprouting from every spot of exposed skin, eased himself out of the armoire and took a few unsteady steps.

"Good heavens," Esme exclaimed when she saw the state of him.

Henny held up a firm palm. "That's far enough. Carmody's a crack shot and it looks like she got you good."

The tiny man tried to brush the dust from his frame, but his fingers and palms were covered in long strands of hair. He finally gave up with an exasperated sigh. The glower he gave the three of us could have stripped the finish off that enchanted wardrobe.

"We've got questions." Henny waved me over.

He was small, hairy, defiant, but I approached him the same way I'd approached one of Ms. Ruthie's boyfriends when I caught him with his hand in the kids' donation jar.

"You're going to tell us what's going on here, Mr. Pyle. Why are you selling fake salamanders, and what's it got to do with Oliver?"

"Pfft." Big Harv crossed his hairy arms. "What makes you think anything has to do with that conniving rat, Oliver?"

"Probably because you just called him a 'conniving rat,'" Henny said.

"Well, he was one. You know that as much as I do. Cocky, conceited, condescending. *That's* what should be etched into that joke of a memorial stone on the Village Green." Big Harv's face flushed red under the long strands of hair, then his eyes darted past us. "Where's Wee?"

"Taking a little nap," Henny said.

Big Harv let out a noticeable sigh of relief.

"Don't change the subject," Henny said. "What were you up to with Oliver?"

He grumbled again, but must have realized there was no way to escape. "Just a little side business. Make some extra cash, that sort of thing."

The two did not make convincing business partners. "With Oliver?" I asked, skeptically.

"It was his idea to begin with. Told me he'd got a lead on some salamanders. Now, even I know that these things can bring in a pretty penny, and I'm not one to pass up a good deal."

Henny grunted. "Go on."

"But we had to move them under the table. Salamanders like these are regulated. There are strict controls. You can't just plop 'em in a shop window."

Benoit's words replayed in my mind. *Marguerite is a protected species.*

"What was the plan if you couldn't sell them openly?" I asked.

Big Harv gave me a look so patronizing that I blinked in surprise.

"You sell them *secretly*," he said. "I've got connections, and I'm not the only one looking to make some money. These things breed. That's the angle we took."

"We?" Esme repeated. "Do you mean you and Oliver?"

Big Harv scrunched up his mouth like he'd swallowed a lemon. "Not Oliver. We as in Wee."

"What happened to Oliver?" I asked.

His mouth contorted again. Through gritted teeth, he said, "After I paid for the salamanders, he decided to renege on his part of the deal."

"Renege?" I asked.

"He said he didn't want to go in on the salamander scheme after all. Didn't pay for his half, didn't do any work. Just left me high and dry with a hundred slithery lizards—"

"Amphibians," Henny corrected.

Big Harv waved his hairy arms. "Whatever they were, I don't care! Oliver left me in the lurch."

"So you killed him?" Henny asked.

At this, Big Harv slapped his mouth shut.

"He left you holding the bill so you killed him." Henny said the statement as fact.

The man writhed against Henny's statement. It was clear he wanted to say something, but held back. Finally, he couldn't hold it any longer and blurted out, "No."

"No?" I repeated. "No to what?"

He crossed his arms and clammed up.

"How about this scenario," I said. "Oliver leaving you with a hundred valuable salamanders was one thing, but Oliver leaving you with a hundred *fake* salamanders worth nothing was another."

His eyes widened, but he remained closed-lipped.

"At least with real salamanders you could have made some money. But fake ones, well, that makes your whole investment a flop. A huge loss, I'm sure."

Big Harv's fists had begun to shake, and the red face had returned. I knew I'd hit the nail on the head.

"Once you realized Oliver had slithered out of the deal, leaving you with worthless stock, you snapped, confronted him, and murdered him because of it."

The redness in Big Harv's face deepened. He was ready to burst.

"You killed him in that alleyway," I said. "And you left him there for us to find."

Visibly shaking, the tiny man stomped his feet. "You don't know what happened and I'll never say!"

Henny pushed forward, an inch away from him. "Why not, Harv? We've caught you red-handed and the facts aren't looking too good. What else have you got to hide?"

What else?

I held up a hand to pull Henny back. "Wait."

She looked back at me, angry herself. "Constable Potts is sniffing in our cauldrons, building his case against us and you want me to wait?"

"Henny," Esme said in her soft voice, "let her speak."

Henny shot her twin a glare, but backed down.

"I don't think it was Big Harv," I said before Henny could seethe further.

"Who then?" she asked.

"It was *Wee Harv.*"

At mention of his son, Big Harv, red-faced and indignant, choked back tears.

I turned to him. "It was Wee, wasn't it? Wee wore the trench coat. He stayed hidden and no one would recognize his voice since he's so quiet."

"No," Big Harv blubbered. "No."

I couldn't relent. "He sold the banana slugs to Mayor Theo, and it was Wee who met with Oliver in the alleyway."

"No, no." But the tiny man withered.

"Tell us the truth," I demanded.

Big Harv wiped his nose with a hairy arm. "It… It wasn't his fault. He didn't understand what I'd said. He didn't understand…" The man's words trailed off into a slew of tears. "He doesn't know his own strength."

"Tell us what happened," I said. "It's over now, you know that."

Big Harv sniffled away his tears and took three heaving breath. "When I found out Oliver's scam, I was so mad. I said we'd lost everything and that I was going to kill him—you know, just saying stuff out of anger. Wee must have heard me, saw how mad I was. He came back to the warehouse that day and told me Oliver wouldn't bother us anymore." Big Harv shook his head solemnly. "It's just him and me, you see? He's all I've got and I'm all he's got. He wanted to save us." The man's voice trailed off into barely a whisper. He collapsed onto the side of the armoire and sunk his hairy head into his hairy hands. "He doesn't know his own strength."

Despite Big Harv's attempted escape, I couldn't help but feel sorry for him. Sorry for Wee, mostly. He just wanted to keep his family safe and together. I knew that feeling.

I glanced at Esme, whose eyes were wet with the beginnings of tears. Even Henny's face, usually so stony and strong, had wilted from Big Harv's story. These two were my family now, and I'd be devastated if I were torn away back to the orphanage, or sent to the drudgery of Crazy Barry's Bargain Basement Brooms.

In one sense, Wee was a victim. Big Harv, although not the actual culprit, had chosen to protect his family instead of go to the authorities.

But I had to keep my family safe, too.

"We should call Constable Potts," I said.

"Oh, dear." Esme's voice was barely a whisper, as though she didn't want to accept the inevitable.

Henny remained silent, which spoke volumes.

Harv's drooping, hairy form remained slumped on the side of the armoire. I tucked a hand into my pocket and pulled out a jar of my hair reversal potion. I stepped forward, kneeled beside him, then placed the jar in his hairy palm. "Sometimes, all we know how to do is protect the ones we love. I can understand that. Take this, at least. It should help."

Big Harv curled his fingers around the jar and nodded his head solemnly. "My poor boy."

Seventeen

That evening, Henny, Esme, and I tried to distract ourselves with tidying the storefront and workroom. Through
sighs and grunts and tsks with the shake of a head, we
managed our tasks with half-hearted effort and a decided
lack of vigor.

By the time Constable Potts had showed up to Big
Harv's Enchanted Imports & Antiques, any remaining
ounce of fight had drained from the small man. We'd left
him there to his fate, along with Wee Harv, whose snores
could be heard echoing throughout the building.

Now we tried to forget. It was easy to scour the town
for clues when you thought a vicious murderer was on the
loose, but when it turns out the only assailant was a gentle
giant protecting the only family he knew, well, that put a
different spin on things.

The doorbell chime broke us from our tidying stu-
pors. I set down the mop bucket and followed Henny and
Esme to the front of the shop.

A frizz of curls poking over the counter greeted us.

"What do you want, Boyd?" Henny asked with her

signature snarl. "And why do you have a suspicious twinkle in your eye?"

Boyd looked around eagerly, finally breaking into a smile when he saw me emerge from behind Esme.

"I got news," he said. "Thought you'd wanna hear."

Esme perked up. "News? About what?"

"'Bout that big fella, Wee Harv."

The three of us exchanged somber glances.

"It's all right, Boyd," I said. "We already know about Wee."

Boyd knit his brow. "But I just come from the Constable's Office. How could you know?"

"We sort of… caught him."

"Caught him? Then you know what he went and told Constable Potts? 'Bout Oliver?"

We nodded in unison.

"Sad business," Esme said, shaking her head. "Best to move on."

"Then you know he told Potts that mean ol' Oliver took a swipe at him? Tried to fight him?"

Henny barged forward, nearly tripping over her bulky shoes, and grabbed Boyd by his grimy collar. "What did you say?"

Boyd went wide-eyed and began to choke.

"Gracious!" Esme fanned herself and rushed to his side. "Release the boy, Henny. Let him speak."

Henny reluctantly dropped her grip on Boyd's collar.

"Go ahead," I said. "Tell us what you heard."

"Yeah," Henny snapped. "Spill it."

Boyd gulped hard. "Well, I were down at the Constable's Office mindin' my own business, you know?"

Henny grunted. "Spying, you mean."

Boyd continued, "Anyway, I overheard Potts say Wee hurt that guy, Oliver, an' asked Wee if Oliver took a swing at him. I don't know why anyone would take a swing at a guy that big, but then ol' Potts asks Wee if this was all a misunderstooding and it was really self-defense."

"And what did Wee say to that?" I asked.

Boyd gulped again. "He just said 'sure.' And that were that."

My eyes lit up. *Self-defense*. It was plausible. Likely inaccurate, but it was Wee's word against…nothing else. And I'd bet the shiniest cauldron the rest of the town would accept Wee's word, too.

"Any word on Big Harv?" Henny asked.

Boyd shook his head. "Nothin' about Big Harv. He were there, all right, but ol' Potts never once asked him any questions."

"Likely a slap on the wrist for concealing evidence," I said. "Unless they get him for fraud."

But relieved as I was that Wee was likely in the clear, the full weight of possibly losing my new family finally hit me. It had been close, but it was over. A lump rose in my throat.

"You okay, Miss Carmody?" Boyd asked. "I ran over here real quick 'cause I knew you been searchin' for the bad guy. Thought you'd be glad to hear."

I tousled the boy's hair. "There's no bad guy, Boyd. Just a big kid trying to keep his family together."

A moment later, a deep rumble shook the potion shop. I grabbed for the counter to steady myself. Through the windows, a few bricks tumbled from the upper stories and smashed onto the sidewalk.

The shaking lasted only a few seconds, then subsided.

"Good heavens, what was that?" Esme asked.

Henny shook her head, her hair more frazzled than ever. "Maybe an earthquake?"

Boyd ran to the door and looked out. "Gosh, everyone's comin' outside."

"Let's go." Henny grabbed my arm and snagged Esme, too, then pulled us out to the sidewalk.

Just as Boyd had said, Chester Hollow's residents were already gathering along Main Street. Some pointed farther down. We follow their directions, Henny leading us zig-zagging through the crowds. We scrambled through the ogling citizens and emerged in front of the portal.

It rumbled again. The entire wall shook. Bits of weathered splintering rained down onto our heads. I shook it away.

"Is it opening?" I asked.

Esme inched back a step. "Oh dear, I hope not."

The shaking stopped, and the last remnants of splinters drifted to rest on the street and sidewalk.

The voices in the crowd behind us drew quiet as we waited for the next eruption. We waited. And waited. But the portal remained silent.

"I think it's over." There was genuine dread still in Henny's voice.

"But what does it mean?" I asked. "Esme said the portal was dormant."

Henny's mouth drew into a sharp line. "It means someone is trying to come through."

The End of Book 1

Lucinda Harrison grew up like most of Gen X: totally feral. She roams the suburban wilds of northern California with her feline accomplices and two house plants that thrive on neglect. She loves to write cozy mysteries with snark and sass and a little bit of soul.

Connect online at lucindaharrisonauthor.com

BOOKS BY LUCINDA HARRISON

Poppy Lewis Mystery Series
Murder in Starry Cove
Best Slayed Plans
A Foul Play
Dead Relatives
Shock & Roll
Bridesmaid Blues
Gingerdead House (novella)

Potion Shop Intern Series
Alibis & Alchemy